THE WITCH
HERSELF

THE
WITCH
HERSELF

Phyllis Reynolds Naylor

ILLUSTRATED BY
Gail Owens

ATHENEUM *1978* NEW YORK

Library of Congress Cataloging in Publication Data

Naylor, Phyllis Reynolds.
  The witch herself.

  The third vol. of a trilogy; the first vol. is
Witch's sister and the second is Witch water.
  SUMMARY: As more people fall under Mrs.
Tuggle's spells, Lynn and Mouse grow more
desperate in their efforts to find a way to stop the
old woman's evil.
  [1. Witchcraft—Fiction] I. Owens, Gail.
II. Title.
PZ7.N24Wk   [Fic]   78–5437
ISBN 0–689–30664–4

for Hannah Raven

THE WITCH
HERSELF

chapter one

The crow was dead, but the cat was alive, and there was still something very much wrong.

Only the night before Lynn had gone outdoors to get another log for the fire and had seen Mrs. Tuggle standing in the street out front. She had been wrapped in a heavy brown coat, almost hiding her face. As Lynn had watched from the shadows, the old woman had pointed one finger at the Morley house, chanted something that Lynn could not understand, and then hurried on up Water Street to her house at the top.

Lynn sat on the window seat in the music room, her chin on her knees, hugging her legs for warmth. The snow outside had settled into a hard icy crust, and cold air seeped through cracks around the bay window. She wiped a clear spot on the frosty glass, but it soon clouded over again.

That was the way it was with evidence. Whenever she and Marjorie Beasley thought they had proof of Mrs. Tuggle's witchcraft, it never seemed clear enough to convince anybody else. That the old woman was eccentric, everyone agreed. There were even rumors that her younger brother, who had supposedly drowned over forty years ago and was buried in the old cemetery, had not died accidentally at all. But beyond that, no one paid much attention to her. She remained a mystery, a conversation piece, a little lady who had come over from England, heaven knew when, and kept to herself in the house on the hill.

Of course, the Morleys would not be involved at all if Mother hadn't gone looking for a studio last year where she could write. She had been looking for a barn, actually, or a loft—the usual sort of place where authors choose to work—when her eye fell on Mrs. Tuggle's old henhouse. Instantly she had seen the nesting boxes along one wall filled with envelopes and paper and carbon sets, and in a few months she had cleaned it out and redecorated it, with the help of the old woman herself.

Outside, a small figure in a blue-hooded coat was coming slowly down the icy hill, and Lynn recognized the skinny legs of Marjorie Beasley, better known as "Mouse." Her piano lesson was undoubtedly over and she was stopping by, as she always did on Mondays, to talk an hour or so before dinner.

Lynn couldn't help but smile as she watched Marjorie's feet skid out from under her on an icy patch, sending her sprawling on the sidewalk and her music flying. But soon she was making her way across the street to the Morley house and starting up the steep steps that led to the front porch. Lynn got up and waited for her at the front door.

"You saw me fall, I'll bet," Marjorie said, taking off her huge owl-like glasses and wiping them on the sleeve of her coat.

Lynn smiled again. "I couldn't help laughing, Mouse. You looked as though you were trying out for the Olympics or something. I mean, your feet were going in all directions."

Marjorie laughed too. "I'm starved," she said, which is what she always said when she came in. It didn't matter if she had just eaten Thanksgiving dinner. Mouse was always hungry, and she never seemed to gain an ounce.

Mrs. Morley was standing at the back door when the girls came in the kitchen. Her arms were folded across her chest as she stared out over the yard and the garden and the fields that led down to Cowden's Creek.

"I hate January," Mrs. Morley said, as if to herself.

Lynn and Mouse stood motionless in the doorway.

"Mother?" Lynn said, and waited.

Mrs. Morley turned around, stared at the girls for a moment as though she hardly recognized them, and suddenly was herself again.

"I didn't hear you come in, Marjorie," she said. "Gra-

5

cious, it's cold out there, isn't it? The streets positively shine they're so slippery. Want some lemon bread? I've just baked a batch, and it's best when it's hot."

Mother looked like a girl herself, Lynn thought, with her hair tied back by a scarf, her sweater pulled up on her arms, and old loafers showing beneath her plaid slacks. What's more, she was pretty, and Judith and Stevie, with their wide-spaced eyes, resembled her. Lynn resembled her father. Their faces were long, the eyes close together. When Lynn looked in the mirror, she seemed to see a young colt instead of a girl, and she was not particularly pleased with the resemblance.

"Thanks," Marjorie said, as Mrs. Morley cut two thick slices of the bread and spread them with cream cheese. "Smells delicious."

They took their bread back into the music room and curled up on the window seat.

"I've decided what I want to be," Mouse said, taking a big bite and catching the crumbs with her other hand.

It was an obsession with Marjorie. Ever since her parents had separated a few months before and her mother had gone to live in Ohio, Mouse craved to know what career suited her best. It was another way of expressing her fears about what would become of her, Lynn decided, and Lynn was very good at figuring people out. What *she* wanted to be was a psychiatrist, and Mouse used to say that all she could think of becoming herself was Lynn's first patient. But now she had something else in mind.

7

"What do you want to be?" Lynn asked. She was prepared for anything where Marjorie Beasley was concerned.

"A hypnotist."

"A *what?* Where did you get that idea?"

Mouse grinned, and the grin made her look very unlike a hypnotist. Marjorie had always looked like a mouse, with her huge eyes and her stubby nose and the short dark hair that framed her face.

"From a book," said Marjorie. "Daddy gave it to me. He got it in a box he picked up at an auction. I'm on chapter two already, and when I finish, I'm going to practice on you."

"That's what friends are for, I guess," Lynn said gamely. "But you know, Mouse, it could be dangerous."

"I won't do anything drastic," Marjorie promised.

"How will you make a career of it? Go on stage?"

"No. I thought maybe I'd work in a dentist's office and hypnotize people who were afraid of the drill. Or maybe I could work with you and hypnotize patients so they could remember what happened to them when they were small."

"Hypnotism can help you remember things?"

"Sure."

"If you had a previous life, Mouse, could you find that out too?"

"A *previous* life! Creeps, Lynn! You mean like maybe you were Pocahontas or somebody?"

"Something like that."

"I suppose you could. Who do you think you were?"

8

"I don't know that I was ever anybody else. I'm just curious, that's all."

They sat awhile without talking. Mouse picked up the last crumb of the lemon bread, which had fallen down on the window seat, and stared out over the frozen snow.

"It's happening again, Lynn," she said at last. "I can feel it."

"What is?" Lynn asked, but she already knew.

"Mrs. Tuggle's up to something. I can just tell."

Like a wisp of cold air, a tingle of fear ran the length of Lynn's body and then ebbed away, leaving her shivering. She had felt it, too. It was just that it became official when Mouse said it.

"What makes you think so?" she asked finally.

"I passed Mrs. Tuggle on the street when I was coming back from my piano lesson. It was the way she looked at me, Lynn. I can't describe it. Her eyes—something about her eyes. She seemed so confident, so sure of herself. And then she called me by a name I never heard before. At first I thought she was going crazy— that she had me mixed up with somebody else. But I'm sure that's not it. There's a reason she talks sometimes in that language no one can understand."

"I feel it, too," Lynn confessed, and told Mouse about seeing the old woman standing in the street the night before. "What should we do, Mouse? What in the world should we do?"

"I don't think we can do anything until we know exactly what she's up to. We'll just have to wait."

9

"That's the hardest of all."

After Marjorie had gone home, Lynn wondered about it again. She was uneasy, but she did not know why; restless without a reason. Every day the family lived its usual routine—Father to work at the courthouse, Mother to her studio, Judith to junior high, Lynn to sixth grade, and Stevie to kindergarten, and yet something was not as it should be, and the something escaped her.

That night at the dinner table, the fear or the dread or whatever it was seemed a little closer, a little more real, when Mother said suddenly, almost casually:

"I'm going to move my studio into one of Mrs. Tuggle's upstairs rooms till spring. That henhouse is just too drafty, and my fingers are always cold in spite of the stove."

Mr. Morley shrugged and went on eating his soup. Judith seemed not even to have heard. And Stevie was forming a circle of peas around the edge of his plate.

"Do you think that's a good idea, Mother?" Lynn asked finally.

"If it will keep me from freezing, I think it's a marvelous idea," Mrs. Morley replied.

"Pass the butter," said Judith.

If she were right about Mrs. Tuggle, Lynn thought, and the old woman *was* a witch who was trying to lure people into her coven, there had to be a reason why she was doing it now. Why would she live peacefully in this little Indiana town for fifty years and then suddenly begin trying to form a coven?

The reason for one witch to try to create others was simple. The more witches there were in a coven, the greater the cone of power. That was what she and Mouse had learned from the book *Spells and Potions* before the cat destroyed it. But why did Mrs. Tuggle want more power at this particular time? Lynn believed it had something to do with the cemetery, but she had no proof.

There were actually two cemeteries in the town, an old one and a new one. Many people felt that the old one, which had long been neglected, should be re-developed and turned into something else, even high rise apartment buildings, and that the graves should be moved to the new cemetery. In checking death certificates of those who were supposed to be buried there, however, the clerk at the courthouse could find no death certificate at all for Mrs. Tuggle's brother. Nor was there, upon further investigation, any record in the county newspaper of a young boy drowning forty years ago.

Lynn felt that there was a reason why Mrs. Tuggle did not want her brother's grave disturbed, a reason why the old woman felt she needed all the power she could get to force the city to leave the ancient cemetery alone. Mouse said that if the coffin were ever dug up and opened, it would probably be empty. *She* believed that forty years ago Mrs. Tuggle had bodily transformed her young brother into her demon cat, the huge brown-black beast that roamed the neighborhood at night and seemed almost human in its responses. And indeed, the cat wore a chain about its neck with a spider medallion, the same sort of medallion that Mrs. Tuggle's brother wore in a photograph that Lynn and Mouse had seen once in the old woman's living room. But because they had no proof, there was nothing they could do.

Later in the week, Marjorie finished reading the book on hypnotism and wanted to try her ability on someone.

"How about Stevie?" Lynn offered, not wanting to volunteer herself just yet. At least this way she could observe what was happening and stop Mouse if it seemed to be getting out of hand.

"Hey, Stevie," Lynn said as her small brother ambled by the living room where they were sitting. "How would you like to be the subject of an experiment Mouse is doing?"

"Okay," said Stevie at once, ready for any diversion. His trust caused a slight pang in Lynn's conscience. "What do I hafta do?"

"Just sit in this chair, Stevie," Mouse instructed, "and make yourself as comfortable as you can. That's it. Lean back and let your legs go limp. Now you've got to pay attention to me, Stevie. Listen to what I say and think about staying comfortable."

Stevie sat motionless, grinning.

Mouse chose a spot of sunlight on the wall and asked him to look at it.

"Don't take your eyes off that spot," she instructed.

"You are very, very tired now. You want to go to sleep. . . ."

"I am not!" Stevie said indignantly, fearing it was all a nap trap. "I'm not sleepy at all!"

"I know, but we're just pretending," Mouse said hastily. "Just *pretend* you're very tired, Stevie, and that you want to go to sleep. Your legs feel heavy, very heavy . . . your feet are heavy. . . ."

For five minutes Stevie sat very still and his eyelids began to droop just a little. At that moment Lynn sneezed, Stevie's eyes popped open, and Mouse had to start over again.

"Your feet are heavy, Stevie, your arms are very limp . . . your eyes are very, very tired . . . you are looking at the spot of sunlight on the wall and feeling very sleepy. . . ."

This time, when his eyes began to droop, Mouse said, "Now you are going to relax your right arm, Stevie . . . don't try to move it . . . just let it do whatever it wants, and it will rise up in the air. Your right arm will bend at the elbow and rise. . . ."

And slowly, as Lynn watched, Stevie's right arm bent at the elbow, rose up in the air, and stayed there, as if held by some invisible string. The fingers of the hand hung limp, and Stevie's half-closed eyes remained on the spot of sunlight ahead of him.

Mouse was suddenly terror stricken at her own power. Quickly she clapped her hands and said, "Okay, Stevie, that's it! Wake up! You're awake now, Stevie. Wide awake."

Stevie's arm went down again, he blinked a few times, and looked at Mouse.

"When are we gonna start, Mouse?" he asked.

"It's all over, Stevie," said Lynn.

"Nothing even happened!" he protested.

"Did you feel your arm rise up?"

He shook his head. Then nodded. He couldn't seem to remember.

Lynn and Mouse stared at each other. It worked! Mouse could do it!

"This is a dumb game," said Stevie, sliding off the chair and going out to the kitchen for some cookies.

"Try me," said Lynn, but Mouse shook her head.

"I'm going to read the book again so I don't make any mistakes," she said. "Wouldn't it be awful, Lynn, if I got somebody to sleep and couldn't wake them up again?"

The following day, however, Mouse came over and said she was ready to try. They went up to Lynn's bedroom, the whole third floor of the Morley house—which she shared with Judith, divided in the middle by a heavy curtain. Lynn lay down on her bed. This time Marjorie had brought a spoon, a shiny silver spoon, that she turned from side to side in her hand as she stood at the foot of Lynn's bed.

"Concentrate on the spoon, Lynn, and just let yourself go. Make yourself as comfortable as possible."

Lynn settled her head on the pillow, wiggled her feet a few times, and lay with her arms outstretched, palms turned upwards, shifting here and there until every inch of her body was relaxed. The spoon in Marjorie's hand was slowly turning this way and that in the dim light of the winter afternoon, the silver alternately gleaming and growing dark again as it twisted one way and then another.

"You are sleepy, very sleepy," Mouse intoned, and Lynn began to giggle.

Mouse stopped. "Listen, Lynn. You have to take it seriously or it won't work."

Lynn tried again. "Okay, I'm ready now."

Again the spoon went up, and Lynn focused on it intently. Back and forth, back and forth, it twisted.

"Your feet are very heavy, Lynn, you can feel your heels sinking down in the bed. Your eyes are tired. Your arms are relaxed. You can barely move them. Your fingers are limp now, and your eyes are beginning to close. You are sleepy, very sleepy. . . ."

At first Lynn thought it would never work. She was much too conscious of Mouse at the foot of her bed looking far too serious and therefore rather silly. The ridiculous spoon went round and round . . . those dumb words. . . . But as the words were repeated again and again, the soft monotony of sounds bored her and her mind began to wander. She felt as though she were floating away from the bed, from the room, from Marjorie. . . .

". . . you are very tired, very sleepy, and you want to rest," came Mouse's voice again and again.

Lynn was floating now, up beyond the ceiling and out over the back yard, hovering over Cowden's Creek.

From her position above the sycamore trees she could see Mrs. Tuggle's house at the top of the hill and the Beasley home at the bottom, with her own in between. She could see the school where she and Mouse went every day and the playground equipment and the business district and library and Mr. Beasley's bookstore. Then she saw the old cemetery, with the iron gates that hung on one hinge and the gravestone of the two angels where Mrs. Tuggle's brother was buried; then she noticed the fog settling in, and it was difficult to see any more, and suddenly someone was slapping her face and she heard Mouse saying:

"Lynn! Wake up! Wake up! It's over, Lynn! You are wide awake now."

She opened her eyes. "Good grief, Mouse, we just got started." She sat up on one elbow. Marjorie's face looked very strange. "What's the matter? What happened?"

"I was afraid you wouldn't wake up."

"How long was I out?"

"Just a few minutes."

"Then why did you try to wake me?"

"I got scared."

"Why?"

"Something you said. . . ."

"*What? Tell* me, Mouse!"

"Well . . . I was going to take you back to when you were five, just for practice," Marjorie said. "But I never got that far."

"Why not?"

"I did everything the book said. I asked if you were comfortable and you said 'yes.' I asked if you wanted to go on a little trip with me, and you said 'yes'. I asked how old you were now, and you said 'eleven'. Then I asked what your name was, and you said, 'Dorolla'."

Lynn stared at her. "I said *what?*"

"Dorolla."

"Who's she?"

"That's what I want to know."

"Well, Mouse, why didn't you try to find out? Why did you bring me out of it?"

"I tried to find out, Lynn. I said, 'Who is Dorolla?' and you just said, 'My name is Dorolla'. That's when I got scared and woke you up."

Lynn looked at Mouse. What did it mean? Where had the name come from? She was sure she had never heard it before in her life.

Mrs. Morley was now working on the third draft of her manuscript about witches. She had begun the book early last summer, rewritten it during the fall, and was now doing the third and final revision.

Ordinarily, third drafts were happy occasions. The writing usually went rapidly and well, and Mrs. Morley was in a good mood. But this third draft was different. The final chapters were not going well at all. Mother seemed nervous and edgy. Sometimes she spoke sharply for no apparent reason. Mr. Morley and Judith noticed it, too.

"You haven't heard a word I said." Father put down

his newspaper and looked across the room at Mother. She was curled up in her big green chair near the fireplace, with her writing board in her lap. In the bookcase nearby were all seven of her published books. *By Sylvia Jackson Morley*, each book said on the cover below the title, and each was an adventure story taking place on the ocean or in the mountains or out in the desert somewhere. Not until now had she ever written a book about witches.

Mrs. Morley looked up.

"I read you a whole story from the paper, and you weren't even listening," Father said again.

"I'm sorry, Dick. I guess I was distracted."

Judith was sitting at the dining room table restringing a strand of beads. Lynn, across from her, was doing her math homework.

"You've been distracted a lot lately, Mom," Judith said. "Every time I talk to you, you seem a million miles away."

"It's this darn manuscript," Mother said, shoving it away from her. "I don't know what possessed me to write a book about witches. It's been nothing but trouble. I've been so bothered with it, I haven't even had time to move into Mrs. Tuggle's."

"Possession, that's what it is!" Father quipped. "Write about witches, and they fly out of the pages and take over."

Lynn kept her eyes on her homework, but she was listening to every word. It was important, however, not to show it. Her suspicions about Mrs. Tuggle had caused one big argument between her parents already, and she didn't want to risk another. Not until she had absolute proof, proof she could hold in the palm of her hand, proof nobody could dispute, would she bring the subject up again. But that didn't mean that she and Mouse weren't working on it.

"I'm paying full attention now," Mother was saying to Father back in the living room. "What were you reading to me?"

"It's a story about the cemetery. The committee investigating land use is supposed to come up with a recommendation by March thirty-first about whether or not to close the old cemetery. Then the zoning commission will decide what to do about the land."

Mother drew her knees up and locked her hands around them. "I certainly don't want to see a high rise built back there, Dick, the way some of the businessmen are proposing. I would hate to look out our back door, across the garden and the meadow, and see tall buildings on the hill across the creek."

"Well, we'll see what happens. Lots of groups are making suggestions. Some want a high rise, some want a shopping center, some want to just keep the cemetery. Mrs. Tuggle, in fact, turned in a petition yesterday with fifty signatures on it asking for just that."

"She did? I've never known her to get involved in local politics. But if it was a choice between those old fallen tombstones and a high rise apartment house, I'd prefer the tombstones, too!"

The following afternoon when school was out, Lynn

and Mouse, bundled in coats and caps and scarves, paid a visit to the old cemetery themselves. In spring, summer, and fall, it was their favorite talking place. Under the huge oak tree at the top of the hill, Lynn would sit down on the gravestone of Mrs. Elfreda Lewis, which had fallen down in front of the tombstone of Mr. Lewis, making a perfect high-backed chair. Mouse always sat across from her on the grave marked "C. L. Pritchard," the grave of Mrs. Tuggle's brother, where two marble angels held a scroll between them. Mouse sat, in fact, on the scroll, and draped her arms affectionately around the angels' necks.

"If they move the cemetery, I'm going to miss our talking place," Mouse said. "I hope Mrs. Tuggle's petition wins out."

"But there's got to be something behind what she's doing," Lynn said. "All these years she's kept to herself, and suddenly she's been standing outside the supermarket getting signatures on a petition. She must have some pretty strong feelings about it."

"Of course. She doesn't want them to dig up her brother's grave for fear the coffin might open accidentally and someone would see that there was no body in it at all," Mouse said. "Maybe there isn't even a coffin. But she'll need more than fifty signatures. Even if most people don't care one way or another. Daddy does, though. He says that if they build a high rise back there, we'll have all sorts of traffic problems, and people will trample the meadow and throw trash in Cowden's Creek."

"But lots of people want the high rise." Lynn leaned forward, resting her arms on her knees as she sat cross-legged on the tombstone. "And Mrs. Tuggle needs help to keep it from happening. Witchcraft, that's what she needs. Listen, Mouse, I want you to try very, very hard to remember that book on spells and potions. You told me once it said that young boys and girls in their teens make the best warlocks and witches because they're so suggestible. But did it say anything at all about adults? If a witch met up with a woman whose imagination ran away with her, is it possible that the witch might try to get her into her coven?"

"Sure," Mouse said. "The book said that a person of any age can become a witch under the right circumstances."

Lynn nodded, as if to herself. "Mouse, did you know that Mother is moving her studio into Mrs. Tuggle's house till spring?"

"Lynn, don't let her do it!"

"How am I supposed to stop her? Could you stop your mother when she moved to Ohio? When parents get an idea to do something, they just do it, that's all. But how do you suppose it would help if Mother became a witch? What could Mrs. Tuggle and Mother do together to stop the city from moving the graves?"

"Lots of things. Accidents. A bulldozer could tip over. The workmen could get sick. The plans could get lost. All kinds of things could keep going on till the city just gave up trying. Mrs. Tuggle could do it, but she'd need as much power as she could get."

For a long time Lynn sat there on the cold tombstone slab. Finally she said, "I wish I could talk to my father about all this—*really* talk to him, I mean. I wish, just for once, he'd believe me."

"It may not be long before he has to believe you, Lynn. If we're right, and Mrs. Tuggle gets to your mother, then your father will see for himself."

chapter two

The next Saturday, Mrs. Morley asked Lynn's help with moving some of her writing supplies into Mrs. Tuggle's house. She would leave her desk and file cabinets out in the studio, she said, but would be taking in several boxes of envelopes, folders, books, and paper. Yes, Lynn said without enthusiasm, she would help.

They set off up the hill, wrapped in layers of sweaters topped with coats. It was only a few degrees above zero, and the icy wind stung their faces, forcing them to stop every so often to turn their backs and catch their breath.

"I've never been so cold in my life, Mother," Lynn said, slipping and sliding on the snowy brick sidewalk that led up past the tall gabled houses to the lone house at the top.

"It's unusually cold for Indiana," Mother told her. "But it shouldn't stay that way very long. Now you see why I can't write in the henhouse. My fingers just don't seem to move."

Mrs. Tuggle's house, like the Morleys', was of modified Victorian design, with three stories, gingerbread ornamentation, gables, and little round windows tucked here and there. There was a porch or balcony that extended around three sides of the second floor, with stairs leading down at one end. The shutters needed paint, but the roof was in good repair, and it looked no better or worse than many of the other houses on the hill.

And yet there was something very different about Mrs. Tuggle's home. It stood apart, for one thing—a wide field separating it from its nearest neighbor. Its front door was completely hidden by a large thornapple tree, and its chimneys stood out starkly against the swirly gray clouds in the winter sky. A brick path led around to the henhouse in back, dividing at one point to branch off toward the barn and tractor shed. No matter how many times Lynn had come up here with her mother, she couldn't seem to take her eyes off that house. How could Mother possibly want to write there?

They reached the burnt-orange door of the studio and went inside. The little potbellied stove sat cold and dead, the rocking chair beside it. Mother's desk was at one end by the cluster of windows, and the file cabinets at the other. A braided rug covered the center of the concrete floor, and the back wall was covered with built-in boxes where all of Mother's supplies were arranged in order.

"I'll need my dictionary and thesaurus," Mother said, putting them into the box, "and that folder over there on my desk. You could begin putting in envelopes and paper, Lynn."

Ten minutes later they had filled two boxes and three sacks with materials Mother felt she couldn't do without and left to take the first load around to Mrs. Tuggle's front door.

Even the door was strange. It was thick and heavy, of solid oak, and there was a huge brass knocker in the shape of a troll with his tongue hanging out. Sometimes, when Lynn stepped up on the porch, she was sure that the troll rolled his eyes in her direction. This time she frowned at the knocker, staring it down. The eyes did not move.

Mrs. Tuggle must have heard them coming, for the door opened at once, and there stood the old woman, waiting for them.

It was not her size that was formidable, for she was a rather small woman, wrinkled and somewhat bent. Her arms were thin, and her bony shoulders stuck up through the sleeves of her housedress, like doorknobs. Nor was it her face, exactly, that caused Lynn to shiver. If one passed her on the street, for instance, she might seem to have a rather grandmotherly face, sweet and gentle. But if one studied her for a long time, as Lynn had done, other features became more noticeable. Mrs. Tuggle's jaw was square and strong. Her eyebrows, unlike the white hair that wisped about her face, were bushy black; and beneath those brows, her eyes were sharp and penetrating—one eye green, the other gray. She looked as though she were capable of producing enormous strength if necessary. Perhaps it was this that frightened Lynn so.

On this particular day, she was wearing a brown print dress, with a gray sweater over it, and a yellow apron.

"Ah, moving day," she said, "I've the second-floor room all prepared, Mrs. Morley. The light is best there, I think, and you've a desk as well."

"This is so good of you," said Mother. "I hope I won't be a bother."

"No one to bother," Mrs. Tuggle said, leading the way upstairs. "Only cat and I are about. 'Tis nice to have somebody sharing the heat when the weather's cold."

She spoke with the accent she had acquired as a young girl in Castleton, on the Isle of Man, and she paid no attention to Lynn at all. There was no love lost between them. Ever since Lynn had come over last fall and accused her, face to face, of witchcraft, Mrs. Tuggle had treated her coldly, with only enough politeness so that Mrs. Morley wouldn't notice.

The second floor room where Mother would be working was near the back on one side. The wallpaper was very old and yellowed, with a strange hexagon print. There was a daybed against one wall, covered with a quilt, a tall dark bookcase with glass doors, a rolltop desk beside the window, with a needlepoint chair, and several small tables covered with assorted knickknacks.

"Perfect," said Mother.

" 'Tis over the kitchen, so it gets extra heat from the oven," Mrs. Tuggle said, opening the blinds a bit wider. "And I've emptied the bookcase so you can put all your things there."

"It will do splendidly," Mrs. Morley said.

"Good, good. Then I will go down and make us a spot of tea while you put your things in order."

She went back downstairs, and again Lynn noticed how quickly she moved, not at all like an old woman, but like some creature who was ageless.

Lynn silently helped her mother arrange her books and supplies in the big bookcase, then went back to the studio for the sacks. When she got up to the room a second time, the cat was standing in the doorway watching her.

He was an enormous animal, with thick brown-black fur. He stood stock still, his tail pointing straight up, the hair on the back of his neck rising stiffly. As Lynn reached the top step with the sacks in her arms, he hissed at her; and when she entered the doorway, he struck out with one paw and scratched her.

Lynn's reaction was instinctive. Swiftly one foot shot out and sent the animal screeching into a far corner of the room.

Mrs. Morley whirled around.

"Stop that!" she rasped, her face strangely angry. She rushed across the room and grabbed Lynn by both shoulders, shaking her hard. "Don't you *ever* do that again. *Ever*. Do you hear me?"

The shaking was so violent that one of the sacks slipped from Lynn's arms and the contents spilled out on the bare oak floor—scissors, tape, pencils, paper. . . .

Lynn stood staring at the mess and then at her mother. Was what she had done really so awful? Mother had never shaken her like that before, not even when Lynn had slapped Stevie! She had never seen such an expression on her mother's face, and it chilled her.

But now Mrs. Morley had turned away and was sitting down, one hand to her head. "I don't know what's the matter with me, Lynn," she said. "I seem to get upset so easily these days. It's just not like me at all, is it?"

Because of the severe cold and the hard snow that had settled everywhere, raccoons had been coming in from the woods beyond Cowden's Creek and rummaging in people's garbage cans. For several weeks in February, residents along Water Street especially had waked each morning to find their plastic garbage cans slashed by the animals' sharp claws, and trash strewn about the yard. In some instances, the raccoons had found their way into garages and basements and were settling down for the cold spell in comfort.

The Humane Society suggested trapping the animals in special cages, which they lent on request. Once the raccoons had been caged, the Society took them to a wildlife preserve in the southern part of the state.

At the end of February, Mouse and Lynn stood in the Beasley backyard and watched Marjorie's father set his trap. Mr. Beasley looked something like an animal himself, for he had shaggy eyebrows and sideburns that matched the color of his curly beard. But he was a gentle man who was fond of his skinny little daughter, and liked having her about.

The trap was a low rectangular cage made of wire. At one end, the door was propped open, and a tasty morsel of food was placed inside at the other end. When an animal crept all the way into the cage and approached the food, his forepaws tripped the catch on

29

the door, and it shut quickly.

"All I have to do then is pick up the cage by the handle and take it down to the Humane Society," Mr. Beasley explained. "Simple and harmless." He set the cage beside his garbage cans, blew on his hands to get them warm, and went back inside, the girls behind him.

"What if you trap a mother raccoon and the Humane Society takes it away to the wildlife preserve?" Mouse wanted to know.

"Then I suppose the papa would come round the next night looking for her, we'd trap him, and the Humane Society would take him to the preserve too. It would be a free vacation for them both."

"What if there were babies?" Mouse insisted. Ever since her own mother had gone to Ohio to live, Mouse was very concerned about families.

Mr. Beasley got an apple from the refrigerator for himself and set a sack of chocolate chip cookies on the table for the girls. "Raccoon babies are born in the spring and are usually out of the nest and on their own before winter," he said. "I wouldn't worry about it, sweetheart."

He went down the hall to his study, and Lynn and Mouse sat at the kitchen table eating cookies. Mouse was still thinking about the raccoons, but Lynn's mind had traveled much further than that.

"Mouse," she said finally, "if Mrs. Tuggle's cat is really her younger brother, bodily transfigured, does it have the brain of a human or the brain of a cat?"

Mouse thought it over. "I don't know. Demons are

supposed to take the form of lizards or birds or goats or something. They're still demons inside, but they behave like the animals they are. I just don't know. It would be part brother, part demon, part cat."

"Under the right circumstances, would it be possible for a demon-animal to talk?"

"The book on spells and potions said they do sometimes."

"Then I've got a job for you, Mouse."

"Like what?"

"Hypnotize the cat."

Mouse stared at her. "You're out of your mind, Lynn. Completely bananas! Just how would you expect me to do that?"

"It's just a chance, Mouse—a long shot—but it's worth a try. I know that Mrs. Tuggle's cat spends the night prowling around in the woods and the old cemetery on the other side of the creek. Mrs. Tuggle once told me so herself. Early each morning it comes back, crossing at the footbridge. I've seen it myself, coming up through the meadow. Let's get up at five o'clock Saturday morning and put the raccoon trap on the footbridge with a bowl of cream in it. If we can catch the cat, you could hypnotize it in the cage."

"Lynn, that's crazy! It would be yowling and carrying on something awful! It wouldn't hold still!"

"At first it might, but after a while I'll bet it would calm down. It would crouch there in the cage watching us with its yellow eyes. Then you could begin talking to it. If the cat's brain is human, maybe it could be hypnotized like anyone else. And then you could ask if its name is C. L. Pritchard and see what it says."

"If Mrs. Tuggle found out we'd trapped her cat, she'd do something awful."

"I intend to tell her, and I'll say we're going to keep the cat locked up till . . . till . . ." Lynn stopped, wondering.

"Till what?" Mouse asked. "Till she confesses to the town that she's a witch? Till the cemetery thing is worked out? How long do you think you can keep a cat in a cage, Lynn?"

"I guess it's Mother I'm really worried about," Lynn said at last. "Maybe I was thinking that we could sort of hold the cat hostage, so Mrs. Tuggle wouldn't do anything to Mom. Okay, Mouse, I guess it was a pretty dumb idea."

"Oh, I don't know," said Mouse. "It sort of grabs me after all. I mean, if I could hypnotize that cat, I'd be famous! My career would be all set. I'd be written up in scientific journals and everything!"

"Slow down," said Lynn. "We don't even have the subject yet."

"Five o'clock Saturday morning, then," Mouse said eagerly. "I'll bring the cage, and you bring the cream."

When Lynn's alarm clock rang at four-forty-five from under a pillow beneath her bed, she flailed wildly at the air trying to find where the noise was coming from and, remembering, turned it off.

She heard Judith grunt and turn over from the other side of the curtain. She lay without moving until she felt certain that Judith was asleep again. Then she crept out of bed, pulled on whatever clothes were handy, as many as she could fit on—several socks, tee shirts, jeans, sweaters—and tiptoed downstairs. She pulled on boots and a coat and a knitted cap and gloves, took the cream from the refrigerator and a bowl from the cupboard, and softly went out the back door.

She didn't know why she had said five o'clock. It was pitch black—as dark as midnight—and the cat would be prowling till dawn. But she had on so many clothes she could hardly walk, and she knew that she would be warm, no matter how long she had to wait.

Five-fifteen came, and Mouse was still not there. Five-twenty. Five-thirty. The rock where Lynn waited was beginning to be cold after all. Then she heard the crackle of brush behind her and saw Mouse in her blue-hooded coat coming down the hill in the pre-dawn, the raccoon cage in her hand.

"It hasn't come by yet, has it?" Mouse asked, afraid she might have missed it.

- "No."

"I woke up, but I was afraid Dad was awake, too. I didn't want to go downstairs till I heard him snoring again."

"What time does he usually wake up?"

"Seven."

"You should be back before then."

They went out onto the footbridge and opened the trap door of the cage. Lynn poured cream from the container into the saucer and carefully pushed it in, as far back as it would go. Then they set the spring and went

33

back to the bushes to wait.

It was warmer sitting on the rock together, sharing body heat. Both of them were sleepy and untalkative, and for one brief moment Lynn felt her head nod as her eyes closed; she had an irresistible urge to lean against Mouse and sleep again. At that moment she felt a nudge.

"Lynn, we were just in time. Look."

Lynn opened her eyes and squinted through the gray fog. Across the creek a dark brown object was making its way down the hill from the cemetery, one paw in front of the other, slowly, sniffing the air as it came. The girls crouched lower, watching through spaces in the bush.

At first they were afraid that the cat would not stop at the bridge but walk on by. It came just to the edge and stopped, sniffing, sniffing, looking around, tail lashing.

"It *knows!*" Lynn breathed. "I'll bet it knows we're here. This will never work, Mouse."

"We'll see," Mouse whispered back. "Be quiet."

Finally the cat sniffed at the bridge itself and then put one paw on the wooden planks, waiting, testing. . . . After another four seconds, it began its low, slinky walk across, head down, eyes glistening in the half-darkness. Closer and closer it got to the trap. Lynn felt her heart pounding wildly.

Then it saw the cage and stopped, its tail erect, head up, ears stiff.

"Oh, lordie!" breathed Mouse. "Will that darn cat never move?"

It moved. It walked all around the cage, sniffing . . . sniffing. . . . Then, testing carefully with one paw, the cat entered the cage slowly, neck stretching, straining to sniff the cream at the other end. The next paw went in, the belly slunk low. The hind feet moved slowly, slowly to the bowl, and suddenly, snap! The metal door clanked behind it and the cat was inside.

A hideous shriek filled the air. It sounded distinctly human. Then the cat was silent. It crouched down in the cage, glaring at the girls who ran down to the bridge. It snarled as they approached and tried to strike out at Mouse as she grasped the handle, but the mesh on the sides and top was too fine for a paw to get through. The cat was no longer interested in the cream.

"We did it!" Lynn said jubilantly. "It worked."

"I've got to get it home and into Dad's car before he wakes up," Mouse said. "I'll tell him I've already checked the trap and there was no raccoon in it. Just before he goes outside, I'll take out the cage and put it on the back porch, and as soon as he leaves for work, I'll bring it in and call you."

"That's a good idea," said Lynn. "Nobody should be able to hear it yowling in a locked car."

She stood watching as Mouse made her way along the creek to her house farther down the row. The cat was strangely silent. When Mouse was out of sight behind the sycamore trees, Lynn started up the hill through the meadow to the Morley's garden beyond, still clutching the carton of cream. Suddenly:

"Where is my cat?"

The words, angry and terrible, seemed to come out of

nowhere. It was as if the sound had come from the gray winter sky itself. Lynn looked up, then around her, and finally turned to see Mrs. Tuggle standing down at the footbridge in her brown coat, a walking stick in her hand, her gray hair flying.

"Where is my cat?" she demanded, and her voice shook. "He always waits for me here at the bridge."

It was the first time Lynn knew that not only did the cat go prowling in the darkness, but Mrs. Tuggle as well. Every night, or perhaps early every morning, they must have gone out together, an old woman and her cat, rushing along wooded paths, past the cold granite stones of cemeteries.

There was no avoiding her question. The container in Lynn's hands and her presence at the creek were all too obvious. There was safety, however, in the distance between them, and somehow, the amount of clothes she was wearing made Lynn feel protected.

"Your cat is being held hostage, Mrs. Tuggle," she said. "As long as my mother is safe, your cat will be safe. But if anything happens to her, you will never see your cat again."

"What nonsense, child! Why would I want to harm your dear mother?"

"You'd just better leave her alone, Mrs. Tuggle," Lynn said boldly, ignoring the old woman's protest. "Don't be surprised if the cat tells me who it is and more besides. Just you be careful, that's all."

With that, Lynn turned on her heels and hurried as fast as she could, short of running, up through the meadow to the garden. But the old woman did not follow. Lynn wondered if she should have said so much, but decided it was time Mrs. Tuggle knew that someone else had power too.

Lynn bolted the kitchen door, put the cream back in the refrigerator, and crept silently up to bed. She had done it. No one knew.

She did not sleep again, but lay very still under the covers, realizing finally how violently she was shivering. Despite her brave words back there on the hill, she was afraid of the old woman. She began to wonder if Mrs. Tuggle knew that Mouse had been there too. Would she know that Mouse had the cat? Perhaps Mouse had never made it back. Perhaps at this very moment she was lying unconscious down by the creek. Perhaps Mrs. Tuggle had rushed up behind her and hit her over the head with her walking stick. Or perhaps the old woman had found her cat in Mr. Beasley's car and rescued him already.

The more Lynn thought about it, the more agitated she became. Finally, at seven-fifteen, she went downstairs to call Mouse. Mother was already up, and making coffee.

"I thought you'd probably sleep late this morning, Lynn," Mother said. "You usually do on Saturdays."

"I'm wide awake," Lynn said. "Thought I'd make some cocoa. It's so cold!"

"It's supposed to warm up a little tomorrow. I certainly hope so. I'm getting very tired of winter, aren't you?"

Lynn settled down in the living room with her cocoa, but when Mother went back upstairs to dress, she dialed Marjorie's number, speaking in low tones so Mother couldn't hear.

"Everything's fine," Mouse assured her. "Dad's almost ready to leave, and as soon as he does, I'll bring the cat inside."

A half hour later, however, the phone rang in the Morley hallway, and Lynn answered. It was Mouse, and she was crying.

"Mouse! What's wrong?"

"Oh, Lynn . . . I never dreamed it would happen. . . ."

"What, Mouse? What?"

"The cat," wept Marjorie. "It's dead."

chapter three

The girls knelt on the kitchen floor of the Beasley home and looked at the cat. It was lying on its side in the cage, and its eyes were half open, vacant, staring. The saucer of cream had gone untouched.

"It was perfectly all right when I took the cage out of the car," Mouse said. "And it was all right when I brought it in the kitchen. I went to the front window to watch Dad drive off, and waited a few minutes to be sure he wouldn't come back for something. Then, when I went to look at the cat again, it was dead!"

"I don't believe it," Lynn said at last.

"Why not?" Mouse whispered back, as though the cat, or someone else, perhaps, could hear. "Dead's dead. I used to have gerbils. And a squirrel conked out on our porch once. I know a dead body when I see one."

"I don't believe it because cats have nine lives," Lynn said, remembering how she had tried to drown the cat last fall, and had been so sure she'd succeeded. "*More* than nine lives. I think it's pretending. The moment we take it out, it will spring to life and run back to Mrs. Tuggle. It's all a trick—a part of her witchcraft, that's what."

"So what do you plan to do? We can't keep it here forever. Daddy will be looking for the trap."

Lynn thought about it. "Wait till three o'clock. If it's still in the same position, we'll take it out and bury it in a sack or something."

"Mrs. Tuggle is going to be furious," said Mouse, leaning back on her heels, her eyes still on the cat.

Lynn nodded. "She'll say we killed it. Do you think she'll do something to Mother to get even?"

"Nothing she wasn't planning to do all along."

"What if she tells Mother we took her cat?"

"I don't think she will. She hasn't told our parents any of the things we've done or said or suspected before. It's between her and us, this battle, and she's out to win it her way." Mouse put her arms on her knees and her chin on her arms and squinted her eyes the way she always did when she was thinking. "I've got another idea, Lynn. You said you told Mrs. Tuggle down at the creek that her cat was being held hostage, and she saw the cream in your hand. She didn't see the cat, but she knew he was around somewhere. You also said you told her not to be surprised if the cat told you something. Right?"

"Right," said Lynn uneasily.

"Okay," said Mouse. "Then I think Mrs. Tuggle killed the cat herself."

"What? Why?"

"So he wouldn't talk."

"But she didn't know where he was! You said yourself that the cat was okay when you brought it in the house. You think she was hiding in here or something?"

"No, I think she did it by witchcraft—by her psychic ties to the demon cat. That's something else I learned from that book on spells and potions. Witches can cause things to happen from a distance by their relationship with other demons. Mrs. Tuggle couldn't release the spring on the cage just by willing it from up there on the hill, but she *could* will the cat's death, because she and the cat are closely connected. And she must have figured that death was better than our having the cat a prisoner."

"But Mouse, she *needed* that demon! She needs all the power she can get! Now she'll be absolutely desperate! She'll do anything!"

"Maybe. But I think she had it all figured out before she killed it, and she'll transfer it to something else. Don't be surprised if a dog shows up here tomorrow or a rat or something . . ."

"Oh, no, Mouse! Don't say it!" Lynn gasped, terrified.

But Marjorie did not seem to find it so frightening. Now that she had figured it out, in fact, she seemed rather proud of herself. She stood up, hands on her hips, and stared down at the animal.

"Let's bury it," she said again.

"No," said Lynn. "At least wait till three. Just in case. . . ."

They put the cage in the pantry and sat down at the kitchen table. Mouse got an orange and divided it between them. Lynn leaned back in her chair, sucking on one of the slices, and found she felt somewhat better herself because Mouse seemed so courageous. Marjorie was much more confident than she had been in the past. Always before, she had waited for Lynn to suggest something to do, listened to what Lynn had to say.

Mouse was a girl who used to daydream in school, who wore socks that didn't match and shoes that didn't lace, and often wore an immense poncho week after week so she wouldn't have to bother with clothes underneath. It was Mouse that Mrs. Tuggle had set her eyes on last fall, like an eagle after prey, and Mouse that Mrs. Tuggle's flock of crows had terrorized. But no more.

Marjorie sat across from Lynn now in a plaid shirt and jeans that fit and with a decent pair of sneakers on her feet. Her hair was combed, and, Lynn realized for the first time, there was something attractive about her face. Good grief, Mouse might even grow up to be beautiful!

"You know what, Mouse?" Lynn said finally. "If Mrs. Tuggle has lived in this town for over fifty years, it seems to me there ought to be somebody, somewhere, who knows something more about her than we do."

"Lots of people have died. Lots have moved. You won't find too many who have been here for fifty years."

"But there must be some. I'll bet if we went around from door to door talking to old people, we'd find out plenty."

"Do you know what our fathers would do if we went around asking questions like that?" Mouse declared. "They'd say we were stirring up trouble and harming an old woman's reputation, and they probably wouldn't let us see each other for a month."

That was absolutely true.

Lynn put her head in her hands and tried to think it through. They had learned from the book called *Spells and Potions* that a witch does not attain her full powers until she has murdered a younger brother or sister. That, they had decided, explained the sudden disappearance of Mrs. Tuggle's orphaned brother when he was sixteen. As a young bride, Mrs. Tuggle had brought him to America with her. He was six at the time and for ten years he had lived with the Tuggles at the top of the hill. And then, he had suddenly disappeared. Mrs. Tuggle had told neighbors that her husband had found the lad floating face down in Cowden's Creek during the big flood. A few years later Mr. Tuggle himself had died, and whatever secrets the white-haired lady had had were now hers alone.

But the girls had learned even more from the old book. If a witch managed to kill someone without any marks of violence on his body—preferably drowning—she could, at some later time, reincarnate him—bring him to life—for the purpose of adding him to her coven. The person could come back as an animal, or as a person. Perhaps the demon spirit in the cat, if Mrs. Tuggle had removed it, would not come back as an animal at all now, but as the boy it had once inhabited. They would have to be very alert.

The morning dragged on. Lynn and Mouse watched television for a while, made some cookies, vacuumed the upstairs, had lunch, anything to keep busy. At two-thirty, Mouse could stand the suspense no longer.

"Let's look at the cat now, Lynn," she said, and they opened the pantry door.

The cage was right where they had left it, and the cat *was* in the same position. Now there was a definite look of stiffness about it, and the eyes had turned a whitish gray.

"It's dead, all right," said Lynn.

They got a burlap sack out of the toolshed. Mouse opened the cage and pulled the cat out. For a moment she paused, then quickly removed the chain with the spider medallion from around the animal's neck and handed it to Lynn. She wrapped the body in the sack, lapping the edges over, until it was a small neat bundle. Then they tied it tightly with rope and took it outside. They chose a place in the meadow and took turns driving Mr. Beasley's shovel down into the hard earth. They could not dig very deep. But at last they had a hole big enough for the cat. They dropped it in, covered it with dirt, and disguised the top with sticks and weeds. The shovel was cleaned off, put back in the shed, and the deed was done.

Lynn couldn't help but notice that the sky was much darker when they finished than it had been at the start of the afternoon.

"Looks like snow again," said Mouse, and they went inside.

It did not snow again, however. On Sunday the wind took on a feel of March, blustery and strong, with a certain wild warmth to it that suggested spring. But Mrs. Morley did not seem to notice that the cold spell had passed. On Monday, she went to work in Mrs. Tuggle's house as usual, silent and preoccupied, and came home the same way.

Father and Judith decided to build a fire in the fireplace after dinner that evening, and Stevie was sent out in the yard to find kindling. The wind had been so strong that small sticks were strewn about all over, and Stevie came back in with his arms full.

"This will *really* start a good fire, won't it, Dad?" he said, dropping the bundle on the hearth. He turned to his mother who was in an armchair. "Did you see all the sticks I got?"

Mrs. Morley did not answer. She was staring at the rug.

"Are you sick, Mommy?" Stevie asked.

Mrs. Morley's eyes focused on the little boy in front of her. "Sick?"

"You act like you're sick!" Stevie insisted. "You hardly ever smile or anything any more."

"What do you mean, any more?" Mother said. "It sounds as if I haven't smiled for weeks."

"You haven't, Mother," said Judith. "You've just been different, that's all."

Lynn, who had been putting dishes away in the kitchen, edged over to the doorway to listen. She watched her father crumpling newspaper to put under the logs in the fireplace, and she could tell, by the look on his face, that he was concerned too.

"You know, Sylvia, I'm having second thoughts about your going to Mrs. Tuggle's every day to write," he said.

"Oh, good heavens!" declared Mother. "Don't tell me that Lynn has influenced you too with her wild stories about the old lady."

"I'm not talking about witchcraft," said Father. "I'm saying that shutting yourself up every day in Mrs. Tuggle's house seems to be having a bad effect on you. Perhaps you're being a little *too* solitary. If you don't associate with anyone but an old lady, it's bound to influence you."

"Is it a crime for her to be old?" Mrs. Morley snapped. "Just because she's been around a long time, I'm not supposed to associate with her, is that it?"

"I didn't say that," Father said firmly. "If you saw plenty of other people during the week and had a more active social life, it would be fine. But you limit yourself to Mrs. Tuggle and her memories and her way of looking at things, and you're bound to be influenced by them."

"So what do you want me to do?"

"Join a club or something. Sing in the choir. Invite people over. Anything to broaden your life a little bit."

Lynn could hardly believe she'd heard correctly. At last Father was beginning to see Mrs. Tuggle for what she was! But she knew better than to say a word about witches. Father hadn't arrived at that point quite yet.

"Well, I suppose I could socialize more after the book is done," Mother said. "I've just started the final draft of the last chapter, though, and I want to stick to it till it's done. Socializing and entertaining now would ruin the effect."

Father didn't answer. They all knew that Mother would do things her own way.

The fire was lit, and Lynn walked in from the kitchen with a box of marshmallows and the long-handled forks. She and Judith and Stevie sat on the rug by the hearth and thrust white puffs into the flames till they caught fire, then blew them out.

"I could never understand why you kids call it 'toasting' marshmallows," said Father, watching from across the room. "Why don't you just say 'burning' marshmallows and be honest?"

"That's when they're best," Judith told him. "Absolutely black on the outside and hot and gooey inside."

"Want one, Mommy?" asked Stevie.

Mrs. Morley held out her hand, and Stevie put one in it. But she didn't even eat it. Lynn wondered if she even saw it sitting there in the palm of her hand.

"Lynn," Mother said after a minute, "Mrs. Tuggle's cat didn't come around all day, and she says it's been

gone all weekend. You haven't seen it, have you?"

Lynn felt the color rise in her face. "The cat? I haven't seen it at all today."

"What about yesterday?"

Yesterday had been Sunday. The cat had died Saturday morning. "No, I didn't see it yesterday either," Lynn said, and her heart pounded for fear her mother would ask about Saturday as well. But Mrs. Morley did not.

"If you see it, let me know," she said. "Mrs. Tuggle is terribly anxious to have it back."

It occurred to Lynn suddenly that the chain the cat had been wearing was still in the pocket of her jeans, and her jeans had been thrown down the laundry chute. Mrs. Morley usually washed clothes in the middle of the week. Perhaps tomorrow. . . .

Later, when Mother was reading a story to Stevie, Lynn got up and went quickly down in the basement. She stopped on the stairs, one hand over her mouth, for the large heap of dirty clothes at the bottom of the chute was gone, and three baskets of neatly folded jeans and shirts and underwear were standing beside the dryer. The wash had already been done.

She rushed over and dug through the pile till she found the faded blue jeans she had been wearing on Saturday. She thrust her fingers in one set of pockets and then the other. Empty. Wildly she opened the washer and dryer, checking each one, then the bottom of the laundry basket, and finally the basement floor. The spider medallion was gone.

Panic rose up in Lynn's chest. She sat down on the stairs, trying to calm herself. Why had they saved it anyway? Perhaps they had been afraid that Mrs. Tuggle would find it and use it somehow if it had been buried with the cat. She must show no obvious emotion or concern when she asked her mother about it. Chances were that Mother had found it in her jeans and set it somewhere. She was always finding things in pockets on wash day.

Lynn took a deep breath and went slowly back upstairs to the living room. She would pick up the comic section of the paper and pretend to read, and after a while she would say casually, *By the way, Mother, did you happen to find the chain that Mouse gave me? It was in my jeans.* Mouse did, after all, hand it to her back there in the Beasley kitchen.

She walked into the living room and over to the magazine rack beside Mrs. Morley's chair to get the paper. And suddenly her eye fell on her mother's left hand. There, wrapped twice around her wrist, almost hidden by the cuff of her sweater, was the demon cat's chain.

Terror overwhelmed her. Lynn stood beside her mother's chair and felt as though her knees would buckle under her, as though the trembling had begun with the soles of her feet. Mrs. Morley wore the evil chain as casually as if she had owned it all her life.

Lynn swayed slightly and leaned against the wall for support. Always before, when she had thought of her mother it had been of someone warm and loving—someone who would understand, and protect her from anything. But lately, it seemed that perhaps Mother had become a part of what Lynn feared the most. Was she one of them, then? Was it already too late to save her from Mrs. Tuggle? Would she have to be saved, instead, from herself?

Lynn went back to the hearth and crouched there beside Judith, watching the flames dance in the black interior of the fireplace. Why had Mother asked her if she'd seen Mrs. Tuggle's cat when she'd already guessed what had happened to it? She had obviously found the chain that afternoon.

The heat from the fire slowly stopped Lynn's shivering. Stevie's happy laughter, as he tumbled about on Mother's lap, sounded all too normal. Perhaps it was all imagination. Perhaps Mother really didn't know that the chain belonged to the cat and had simply put it on so she would remember to ask Lynn about it. After all, Lynn had seen the cat sit on her mother's lap now and then, and had watched her mother stroke its back, but she had never seen Mrs. Morley really play with the animal or explore its fur the way Stevie did. If Stevie saw the medallion, however, he would ask about it at once. He knew it had belonged to the cat. And if he did ask, Mother would realize, if she didn't already know, that Lynn had something to do with the cat's disappearance. She felt relieved, therefore, when she heard her mother instruct Stevie to go get his pajamas on. She would ask her mother about it after he went to bed.

"Want another marshmallow, Lynn, before I put

them away?" Judith asked.

Lynn shook her head, and Judith took the sack and the sticky forks out to the kitchen. Stevie came downstairs again to kiss his parents goodnight, then he disappeared also. Lynn was alone in the living room with her parents.

"Mother," she said after a minute, her eyes still on the fire, not quite daring to look her mother in the face. "Mouse gave me a medallion on a chain, and I've lost it. Have you seen it?" Could her mother detect the shakiness in her voice, Lynn wondered.

"Why, yes I have," Mrs. Morley answered, and held out her left wrist. "Is this it? I found it in the clothes dryer this afternoon."

The medallion dangled in front of Lynn's eyes.

"That's it," said Lynn. "I didn't know what had happened to it."

Mrs. Morley unfastened the chain and examined the medallion in her hand.

"It looked familiar to me somehow, and I just couldn't remember where I'd seen it," she said.

"You've probably seen Mouse wearing it," Lynn said, taking it from her mother. "She has a lot of weird jewelry."

"Maybe so. Well, I'm glad I found it then."

It had been far easier than Lynn had imagined. Mother had willingly given it up. Lynn felt tremendously relieved. Tears came to her eyes as she realized that she had not been really truthful with her mother that evening. She longed to return to the loving relationship they had once enjoyed. If only she could tell her mother everything, hold nothing back. But that was impossible now.

She snuffled once and gulped back the tears. Finally, as the fire began to die out and only the embers remained, Lynn got up from the warmth of the rug and prepared to go to bed herself.

"I love you, Mom," she said as she leaned over to kiss her mother.

"Love you too, dear," said Mrs. Morley.

But as Lynn started up the stairs, she could see her mother still sitting in the same position she had been sitting in all evening, feet tucked beneath her, staring vacantly into the fireplace. The uneasiness returned like a large lump in the throat.

She had hardly reached the landing when the phone rang and her father called her back down. It was Mouse.

The voice at the other end of the line was breathless, excited, and so soft it was difficult for Lynn to understand her.

"Lynn," Mouse whispered. "Are you alone?"

"Well . . . no. I mean, uh . . . not really."

"Okay, then, I won't try to tell you everything. . . ."

"What, Mouse? It's hard to hear you."

"I can't talk very loud because I don't want Daddy to hear. Listen, Lynn, we've got to meet at the cemetery tomorrow after school. We've got to talk some place where it's private."

"Okay. What's up?"

"I found something. I was helping out at the bookstore this evening, and I found something terribly important. It's the most important piece of paper you can imagine."

"Ye gods, Mouse, what *is* it? The Declaration of Independence?"

"Practically," said Mouse. "Uh-oh. Dad's coming downstairs now. I can't say any more."

"Listen, Mouse, show it to me on the way to school tomorrow."

"I can't. I'll be carrying it in my shoe to be sure it's safe."

"The Declaration of Independence, and you've got it in your shoe?"

"I have to, Lynn. If . . . somebody knew I had it . . . well, so long, Lynn. I'll see you tomorrow."

Lynn went slowly upstairs, took a long bath on the second floor, and then went on up to the huge bedroom on the third. What on earth could Mouse have found that Mr. Beasley didn't know about? Whatever, she'd have to wait till the next day to find out.

She put the spider medallion in a corner of her top dresser drawer. She must never let Mrs. Tuggle see it, or Stevie or Judith either, because they would recognize it too and wonder how she got it. And yet she felt a strange fascination for it. In her drawer it became a magnet somehow, drawing her to it. She turned her back to her dresser and fell asleep.

Several times during the night, however, she wanted to get out of bed and touch it, put it on and wear it. But she didn't. She was instinctively afraid. The medallion was evil, she was sure, and were she to wear it—well, she did not even want to think about it.

But sometime in the night she had a terrible dream. She dreamed that people were calling her, only they were not saying, "Lynn," they were calling "Dorolla." She dreamed that she had risen from her bed and gone to the window, and in passing her dresser, she had looked in the mirror and seen not her own face, but the face of the cat. She screamed.

The next thing she knew, Judith was standing over her, shaking her, and the bed lamp was on.

"Lynn," Judith was saying, "I think you've been having a bad dream."

Lynn rolled over and hid her face in her pillow. "I guess I was," she said. "Thanks for waking me. Gosh, it was awful."

"Monsters and stuff?" Judith asked sympathetically.

"Worse. Dorolla."

"What? Who's that?"

"I don't know," said Lynn, "but whoever she is, she's awful."

chapter four

Lynn could tell, as soon as she saw Mouse the following morning, that her friend had something in her shoe. She walked with her foot at an odd angle.

"Mouse, you can't go around all day like that," she said, hurrying down the long flight of steps that led to the sidewalk below. "You'll be crippled by three o'clock."

"It's got to stay right here until I turn it over to the district attorney," said Mouse mysteriously.

"The district attorney? What on earth did you find?"

"Three pages out of a diary," said Marjorie.

"Whose diary? Mrs. Tuggle's?"

"Bertha Voight's diary, that's who."

The excitement that Lynn had felt earlier fizzled out.

"Big deal. Who's she?"

"Who *was* she," Mouse corrected. "Somebody who lived in this town when Mrs. Tuggle was a young woman."

Lynn stopped in her tracks. "What did she *say*, Mouse? *Tell* me!"

Marjorie had to go back to the beginning. She liked a good story, and she hated to give the climax away so quickly.

"Well, last night I was helping out at the bookstore," she began as they resumed their walk up the hill, "and I was writing down all the titles and copyright dates of books that Daddy bought at an auction of the Voight estate. When I opened one of the books to look for the copyright—it was a book of poems by Longfellow—I found these pages folded inside the cover. I could tell they had been torn out of a notebook, and naturally I was curious. . . ."

"Keep *talking*, Mouse!" Lynn cried, hardly letting her stop for breath.

"I took one look at the handwriting and decided it wasn't worth the trouble—it's all flowery, you know, with little circles and curls and stuff—but just as I was about to fold the pages up again, I noticed the word 'Tuggle' so I started reading. She *knew* her, Lynn, and the pages are all about Mrs. Tuggle. Bertha Voight suspected that Mrs. Tuggle was a witch."

"Oh, Mouse! It's just what we need! I'll never be able to wait till three o'clock."

The morning at school seemed to drag endlessly.

Lynn was tempted to make Mouse take the papers out of her shoe at lunchtime so she could read them then, but some of the other girls had sat down beside them in the all-purpose room. She knew that if she and Mouse tried to go off by themselves and read something secret, the other girls would suspect that the papers were love notes from boyfriends and try to snatch them away. No, she would have to be patient and wait till they went to the cemetery later.

On their way to music class, however, Lynn walked beside Mouse in the hall.

"Did she just die?" Lynn asked.

"Who?"

"Bertha Voight."

"I don't know. Somebody's always dead when there's an auction, but she could have been dead a long time. It just means that her relatives were tired of storing all her stuff year after year and decided to auction it off. Daddy always goes to auctions and buys old books. He says if he gets one rare book from somebody's whole collection, it's worth it."

"We've got to go hunt up the relatives," Lynn said.

"What? And show them the papers from the notebook?"

"No. We don't even have to mention them. Let's just go find people who were real close to Bertha and see if they remember anything that happened between her and Mrs. Tuggle—anything she might have told them. It's worth a try."

By three o'clock, Mouse was actually limping. The

teacher wanted to send her to the school nurse, but Mouse said it was merely a darned place in her stocking and that she would change her socks as soon as she got home. Then she set off for the cemetery with Lynn.

It was the first day of March, and the sun beamed brightly down on the streets that had been frozen with snow only a few weeks earlier. The trees were still bare and budless, but they stretched their limbs joyfully toward the warm sky, and shook themselves in the wind.

When the girls reached the old rusted gate of the south entrance, Mouse leaned against Lynn and said, "I can't go another step. I've got to take my shoe off right here." And she did. Clutching the papers in one hand and dragging her unlaced shoe, she went up the hill to the top where the huge oak tree stood sentinel over the graves below. They sat down in their conference place—Lynn on the gravestone of Mrs. Elfreda Lewis and Mouse on the scroll between the angels over the grave marked, "C. L. Pritchard."

"See if you can make out the writing," Mouse said, handing the notebook pages to Lynn and leaning back in the angels' arms, smug and self-satisfied from doing such a marvelous piece of detective work.

The handwriting *was* flowery, and it didn't help any that the papers had been in Marjorie's shoe all day. The sheets were matted together and had begun to tear along the creases. Lynn opened them carefully and spread them out in her lap.

". . . *and sure she suspects that I know more about*

59

her than she would like. . . ." The first line read, beginning in mid-sentence. *"It was Haggerty's mule that led me first to think it. He keeps the beast tied up outside the feed store afternoons while he amuses himself with the men inside, talking and telling stories, as idle men will do. Most of the young ladies in the town take a four o'clock stroll when the air is mild. Whenever Elnora Tuggle walks by the poor animal, his ears lay back and he snorts and jerks as though his very brain is affected. I have seen her cross over now before she passes the mule, so that no one will notice how he takes to her.*

"I've read that the witches of England have long had special power over animals, and Elnora, as we all know, came from Castleton on the Isle of Man, with her new husband and that poor young brother of hers with the constantly sad face. My heart grieves when I look at him. There are no companions his age anywhere about. . . ."

Lynn was reading slowly, jerkily . . . stumbling over words as she tried to decipher the elegant handwriting, and guessing at words in places where the ink was so faint as to be unreadable. The account continued, about how Mrs. Tuggle's husband worked hard tending to his small farm at the top of the hill and probably did not know what his wife was up to.

". . . But I have observed other things as well," Bertha Voight had written on the last of the pages, *"and thinking of them makes my flesh fairly creep. I have seen E. T. talking to the crows and have seen them obey her. She talks in another tongue, not like any on*

earth. Most certainly it is not Italian or French. She is assuredly a spiritualist of some dark sort, but I will keep my suspicions to myself for the moment. Perhaps, if I am observant, I will learn even more. And it comforts me to know what is constantly in my apron pocket. . . ."

Lynn quickly flipped the pages over. "Is this all?"

"That's it," said Mouse. "I looked through all the rest of her books to see if there were more notebook pages around somewhere, but there weren't."

Lynn was disappointed. "Mouse, this doesn't tell us anything, really. It's all suspicions, just like ours. We don't even know what was in her apron pocket, for heaven's sake."

"But she's somebody else besides us who suspects Mrs. Tuggle," Mouse said, pouting because Lynn did not make a big fuss over her discovery.

"Well, it's a lead, at least. Maybe we can find some of the Voight relatives and see what they can remember. But please keep those papers somewhere else, Mouse. If we are ever called to present evidence in court or something, you don't want to sit up there on the witness stand and take your shoe off."

Harold Voight was in his eighties. Mouse had casually inquired of her father whether Bertha Voight had living relatives, and Mr. Beasley told her that she had some living in Muncie and an older brother down on Elm Street behind the Baptist Church. Lynn and Marjorie paid a visit on Thursday after school.

It was a large house that had been turned into apartments, and Mr. Voight occupied a few rooms on the first floor. When the girls knocked on the stained glass door on the right side of the entrance hall, they heard the slow shuffle of steps coming toward them, and at last the door opened. An old face peered out at them, flecked with brown age spots here and there. He beat his gums together once or twice before he spoke.

"What do you want, girls?"

"Mr. Voight?" said Lynn, "I'm Lynn Morley, and this is Marjorie Beasley. We're collecting information about how our town was fifty years ago, and we wondered if you could help us out."

"Eh?" Mr. Voight looked at them more closely and then opened the door a little wider. "A history project, eh?"

"Something like that," said Mouse.

"Well, now you come on in here, then," said Mr. Voight, beginning to warm to the idea. He shuffled over to the couch, fussing around with the crumpled cushions and throwing newspapers on the floor so that the girls could sit down. "Want to get a good grade in school, eh? Well, that's good. That's good."

Lynn and Mouse sat together on the couch. A bird in a cage by the window was trilling away, and the sun made a square of gold on the carpet. The apartment had the look of being lived in a very long time by a man who knew where everything was supposed to be. Mr. Voight started to sit down, then remembered something and shuffled out to the kitchen, returning

with a box of peanut brittle, which he offered to them. Each girl took a piece and sat nibbling politely.

"Now, then, what sort of things does your teacher want you to find out?" he asked. "I've been in this town since I was four years old. My folks came from Minnesota, and after they passed away, my brother married and moved to Muncie and my sister and me, we stayed in the family home up there on Maple Drive. Yep, we seen a lot of changes in this town."

"I don't suppose there were half as many houses then as there are now," Mouse began.

"Land sakes, no. Why, most of the houses was down here near the business district, and of course Maple and Elm, well, they was pretty much developed. But Water Street was all meadow, then—hardly any houses at all. Then that English woman came over . . . what's her name?"

"Tuggle?" Lynn said, expectantly.

"That's it. Mrs. Tuggle, she come over and picked out that spot top of the hill for their place. They say her husband wasn't too keen about it, land wasn't too flat up there for plowin' and such, but she had her heart set on livin' on a hill, so they bought the property and built a house. Tried to make it look like the ones down here, you know—gables and such. Used to be they was nothin' but an old dirt road goin' up there, too. Then other folks started buildin' houses along the road goin' up, and they all made *their* houses the old fashioned kind, you know, to match Mrs. Tuggle's. Finally somebody called it Water Street on account of the creek behind, and put in brick sidewalks. Yep, lots of changes since I was a lad, I can tell you."

"Did your sister know Mrs. Tuggle very well?" Lynn inquired.

Mr. Voight scratched his head. "Well, now, that's sort of hard to say. Bertie, she didn't git along real well with anybody, to tell the truth. She didn't even git along sometimes with me. Always naggin', always suspectin' the worst. Oh, I don't mean to say she was always like that—she had her good points. But Bertie was against wickedness of all kinds, and she was always seein' evil where nobody else could see it, you know. Said she had a 'gift'. Used to say there was a battle goin' on in this town between good and evil, and Bertie, of course, was always on the good side. And there was people that Bertha took a dislike to. One of 'em was the Tuggle lady. They was both young women in those days, only difference was Mrs. Tuggle was from England and had herself a husband and Bertie hadn't been nowhere at all and no husband neither. So I suppose maybe it was natural she would envy Mrs. Tuggle some."

Mr. Voight quit talking for a few moments and was very quiet.

"It was more than envy, though," he said at last. "There was somethin' about Mrs. Tuggle that bothered Bertie—she never did say what. Used to go talk to an old priest about it sometimes, and she told me he gave her some kind of protection. I asked her once—came right out and asked her what she had against the

English woman and what it was the priest gave her, but she just clammed up. Wouldn't tell me. 'You'll find out some day,' she says, 'when I decide to tell it'." Mr. Voight shook his head. "But of course she never did tell it, whatever it was. Just two personalities, I guess, that didn't get along."

"Did you know the Tuggles?" Mouse asked.

"Oh, I went up the hill once to help Sam Tuggle mend his fence after Haggerty's mule got loose and kicked the daylights out of the Tuggles' front gate. Seemed like that confounded mule had a grudge against everybody, 'specially the Tuggles. No, they kept pretty much to themselves, same as we did. Folks down here near the business district was sort of one group, and the folks up on the hill was another, and first thing we knew, there were sort of neighborhoods all over the place, 'stead of one big neighborhood like it was when I was a lad. The way the town was laid out then, see, there was this street here that ended back by the firehouse, and on up the next block was the old school, and then on down past the library. . . ."

Lynn and Marjorie couldn't walk out on him now. He had told them what they wanted to know about the Tuggles, and he obviously wanted to talk a lot more. So for another forty-five minutes, they sat on the couch and listened to the bird and munched peanut brittle, asking an occasional question out of politeness.

There was really no new information, Lynn decided as she settled back against the cushions and listened to Mr. Voight drone on and on. He had merely confirmed what Bertha had said in her notebook—that she suspected Mrs. Tuggle of witchcraft, but she had told no one except the priest her suspicions, not even her brother. And the priest, if he was old back then, was undoubtedly dead by now.

When the clock chimed five, the girls leaped up and exclaimed over how late it was and thanked Mr. Voight for his time. He followed them out to the front steps.

"If you need any more information, you just come to me," he said. "Why, I'm practically the town historian. Nothing happened here I can't tell you something about."

Lynn started down the steps, but Mr. Voight's last remark made her stop.

"By the way," she asked, turning around, "do you remember when Mrs. Tuggle's young brother drowned?"

"'Deed I do," said the old man, and he looked sad. "That was the spring of the big floods all over the state of Indiana. The Wabash was flowin' ever which way, and every river and creek in the whole dang state was on the rampage, takin' homes and people with it. I remember bein' down at the general store and hearin' that Sam Tuggle said he'd found the lad face down in Cowden's Creek. Kid was just one of the people the flood took that year." He was quiet again, his eyes on the ground.

"Was there a funeral for him?" Mouse asked.

"That I can't say," the old man said. "Reckon there was, but I didn't go to it. You see, I had my own troubles then, so I didn't pay much attention to what other folks was doin'. That's when Bertha disappeared, you know."

Mouse and Lynn stood staring at the old man in the doorway.

"Yep, the flood took her, too. She went out that mornin' to go look at the creek the way other folks was doin', and she never came back. We figured she leaned too far over and fell in, same as what happened to the Tuggle boy, only her body was never found."

They sat on the steps of the library, across the street from Mr. Beasley's book store, and thought about Bertha Voight.

"She *knew*," said Mouse at last.

"And Mrs. Tuggle *knew* that she knew," Lynn added. "She disappeared, and everyone just assumed she'd drowned in the flood. Even her brother thinks that's what happened to her. What do *you* think happened, Mouse?"

Marjorie leaned back against the railing. "Maybe she was turned into a crow or something. Maybe that big bird you killed last fall was really Bertha Voight."

"Good grief, Mouse! Don't say that!"

"It wasn't your *fault*, Lynn!"

Lynn was quiet a moment. "And the cat?" she said finally.

"That's not our fault either. No cat ever died just from being locked in a cage for a couple of hours."

They were silent again.

"Mouse, do you ever get the feeling that we're next?" Lynn asked at last.

"What do you mean?"

"The demon cat is dead, and so is the crow. And all because of us. Bertha Voight disappeared because she knew too much. If we ever met Mrs. Tuggle alone some night in a dark alley, she'd. . . ."

"It wouldn't have to be night, and it wouldn't have to be a dark alley," Mouse put in. "When she decides to get rid of us, she has plenty of other ways."

"How?"

"I wish I could remember. If the cat hadn't torn up the book on Spells and Potions, we could read it and predict what she might try next."

"*Please* try to remember, Mouse."

"I just can't, Lynn. There was something about . . . a charm that could be used to control somebody, but I don't know any more about it."

They huddled there on the cold steps, watching the people pass in front of them on the sidewalk. The customers going in and out of the bookstore, the women who stopped to chat with each other . . . the town, on this early March day, seemed to go on the same as before. The one woman who might have warned everyone about Mrs. Tuggle had disappeared. How many other things had happened, Lynn wondered, that had been dismissed as mere coincidence? How long could a witch go on controlling a town without anyone knowing about it? Mrs. Tuggle looked as though she could live forever. Was it possible that she had already controlled far more than anyone realized—that she might even be able to control people's minds?

"Mouse," she said. "I want you to hypnotize me again.

But this time, after I'm hypnotized, I want you to call me Dorolla and see what happens."

"Lynn, I'm too scared."

"Why should you be if I'm not?"

"Because I don't like the thought of it. I don't like the name Dorolla. It gives me the creeps. It seems evil and awful."

"*Please*, Mouse. If there was something evil and awful in you, wouldn't you want to know more about it?"

"No. I would want to stay peacefully ignorant the rest of my natural life."

"Listen, Mouse. I'm afraid for my mother. Something terrible may happen to her some day at Mrs. Tuggle's. We've got to find out all we can. Hypnotize me one more time and call me Dorolla, and I'll never ask you to do it again."

On Saturday afternoon, then, the girls went up to Marjorie's bedroom for the session. Lynn sat on Marjorie's bed, propped up on pillows, and Mouse sat beside her, gently swinging a gold locket back and forth.

"It's not working, Mouse," Lynn said disappointedly after twenty minutes had gone by. "I'm just getting dizzy, that's all. Try a spoon instead."

So Mouse got a spoon and held it up before Lynn's eyes.

"You are very comfortable, Lynn," Mouse intoned patiently, "and very, very tired. Your head feels very heavy . . . your eyelids are heavy . . . slowly your eyes are closing. . . . You can feel your legs going limp, and your arms are going limp. . . ."

Lynn's mind began to stop its frantic rushing from one subject to the next, and she let her shoulders sag against the softness of the pillow. She felt her eyelids start to close, blinked, and then gave in to let them shut.

"Remember," she heard herself saying after a bit, "to . . . call me . . . Dorolla . . ."

When she opened her eyes again, the room seemed to have grown darker, and at first she could not understand where she was. When she realized that she was at Marjorie's, she thought perhaps she had spent the night, for a long stretch of time seemed to have elapsed. As she sat up and looked around, however, she saw Mouse standing in one corner, her back to the wall, eyes huge.

"Mouse?" she asked.

"Oh, Lynn!" Mouse dropped weakly down on the bed, and her face was pale. "I'll never do it again! I swear, I'm through with hypnotism forever!"

It had worked, then. Mouse had hypnotized her. "What happened?"

"You don't remember anything at all?"

"Of course not."

Mouse looked at her hesitantly, and then took a deep breath. "I put you to sleep. And then . . . I . . ." She shivered. "Oh, Lynn, I'll never do it again!"

"What, Mouse? What happened? *Tell* me!"

"Then I . . . I called you Dorolla instead of Lynn, like you said."

"And . . .?"

"I said, 'Dorolla, how old are you?' For a long time you didn't answer. Once or twice you opened your mouth like you were going to speak, but you didn't. So I asked it again, and then you said, 'I am ageless'. Just like that."

Lynn stared at Mouse. That didn't sound like something she would say at all.

"Then I asked, 'Do you know Lynn Morley?' and you said, 'I am a part of Lynn Morley'."

Goose bumps rose up on Lynn's arms and traveled down her back. "D . . . Did I say anything else?"

"Well, I didn't know what to ask next, so finally I said, 'Tell me about yourself, Dorolla,' and you said, 'You know me already, but you do not know my strength.' Then you said something about being Lynn's opposite. No, I guess you called it, 'Lynn's other side'."

"Oh, Mouse!" Lynn said, and fell back against the pillows.

"So I said, 'Dorolla, do you have anything to do with Mrs. Tuggle?' And you sat straight up and bared your teeth at me, just like an *animal,* Lynn! I was terrified! So I yelled, 'Lynn, wake up!' You lay back down but for a long time you didn't wake up. Oh, Lynn, I was so scared!"

"How long have I been here?"

"About thirty minutes."

"It seemed like a whole night. And I don't remember any of it."

"Lynn, I don't want to be a hypnotist! I don't want to find out all this stuff! I don't want to dig up Dorolla any

Check Out Receipt

Hayner PLD - Alton Square Branch (HYAP-ZED)
618-462-0677
www.haynerlibrary.org

Saturday, June 1, 2019 9:54:31 AM
STIRNAMAN, VIRGIL H

Item: 0003006051429
Title: A shocker on Shock Street
Call no.: jF STI
Due: 06/15/2019

Item: 0003000975692
Title: The witch herself
Call no.: jF NAY
Due: 06/15/2019

Total items: 2

You just saved $14.94 by using your library. You
 have saved $14.94 this past year and $1,370.09
since you began using the library!

Thank You!

more. I don't care who she is. I just want to live a normal life. I want to grow up and raise horses or something. I want to see the Grand Canyon and visit Mexico and forget all about Mrs. Tuggle. If we don't stop this, we'll never get out of Indiana alive."

"If we stop investigating, Mouse, we won't even *grow* up! Mrs. Tuggle will control us all!" Lynn said determinedly. "I understand it now, Mouse! I do! Dorolla is the evilness in me, just as there is evilness in everybody! People have always been a mixture of good and bad, you know that. Only Mrs. Tuggle has a way of communicating with this evilness. She tried it once on Judith but it didn't work, and she's trying it now on Mother. She wants to make the Dorolla in me stronger too, but she won't do it, Mouse! I won't let it happen! As long as I know, as long as I can fight it, Dorolla doesn't have a chance!"

chapter five

There was no school the following Tuesday because all the teachers were attending a workshop.

"I'm going to wash my hair and read a book and just laze around," Judith announced that morning, coming down to breakfast just as Mr. Morley was leaving for the courthouse.

"It's starting to get warmer outside," Father said, carrying his plate to the sink, "I'd think you'd want to go out hiking and see if you could find some pussy willows along the creek."

"Maybe," Judith mused. "I suppose I could take Stevie with me."

"That would be a good idea." Mr. Morley glanced at his wife who sat bundled in a heavy robe at one end of the table, slowly sipping her coffee, her face turned toward the window. "Maybe Lynn could help you move your writing things back to your studio, Sylvia. It's warm enough now, I think. Spring is in the air. You can feel it."

"In a few weeks," said Mother. "I'm almost through with my book. Then I'll move back into the studio."

Mr. Morley paused as though he were about to say something more to her, then stopped. He bent over, kissed her goodbye, and left. Lynn, who had been making toast at the counter, took the cinnamon jar with her and sat down beside her mother.

"I'd like to go up to Mrs. Tuggle's with you today," she said. "I promise I won't talk and disturb you. But I could file or go over clippings or something."

Mrs. Morley turned and smiled at her. "I don't have much for you to do in Mrs. Tuggle's house. It's the studio that needs straightening."

"Let me go with you anyway, Mother. You said you had a whole envelope full of notes and things on witchcraft, and you needed them pasted in a loose leaf binder where you could find them easily."

"I did, but my book is almost done now. I won't need the clippings after that."

"But you might, Mother. You might do another book on witches some day, and then everything would be in order."

"Oh, I suppose so, if you're really looking for something to keep you busy. It would be more to the point, I think, if you stayed home and cleaned out your closet.

75

But you can come if you like."

When Mother went back upstairs to dress, Judith faced Lynn across the table.

"Something's wrong with her," Judith said. "I don't know what it is, but something's just not right. Dad told me that if she doesn't seem any better by April, he's going to have Dr. Thomas come by the house and check her over."

"I don't think she's sick," Lynn ventured. "I think it's Mrs. Tuggle."

For once Judith did not laugh at the idea. "I wish she weren't working up there any more," she agreed, "but I don't know why."

There were light footsteps on the stairs, and Stevie came into the kitchen in his stocking feet, still in pajamas, but wearing an enormous old hat that Mr. Morley used to wear on fishing trips.

"What are *you* supposed to be?" Lynn smiled, pouring his cereal for him and slicing banana over it.

Stevie grinned. "It's my detective hat. Daddy said I could wear it."

"You're working on a case, huh?"

"Yeah." Stevie climbed up in his chair and tucked his feet under him. "Mrs. Tuggle hired me."

Lynn stood still and looked at Stevie.

"To do what?" Judith asked.

"To find her cat. She said if I found him, she'd give me a whole dollar. And she said if I didn't find him but found out what happened to him, she'd pay me fifty cents."

Lynn busied herself clearing up the counter. "So

where do you think you'll look?"

"I don't know. I'm gonna knock on all the doors on this street and ask if anybody's seen a big brown cat."

Lynn felt a tinge of guilt when she realized all the work Stevie was going to do to find out nothing. But her heart stood still when she heard him say:

"I'm gonna ask everyone if they've seen a cat with a chain around its neck with a thing on the end that looks like a spider. Mrs. Tuggle said even if I didn't find the cat but I found the chain, she'd give me a dollar anyway."

He remembers it, Lynn thought. *If he just won't mention it to Mother!*

"I was going to go for a hike along the creek, Stevie," Judith told him. "Want to go with me? Maybe we'll see the cat back in the woods somewhere."

Lynn went upstairs to put on her jeans, and checked to make sure the chain was still in her top dresser drawer. Then she went downstairs, threw on her coat, and went outside with Mother.

The sky overhead was definitely March. It was clear and blue, and the white puffs of clouds were moving rapidly in the force of the wind, making Lynn dizzy as she watched them sailing by. The air was still cold, but the sun was incredibly warm on the back of her neck, and she trotted down the steps to the brick walk below and then began the long climb beside Mother to the house at the top of the hill.

Usually, when Mother and Lynn were alone, going somewhere together, Mrs. Morley made the most of the time, asking Lynn questions about school or Marjorie or her feelings about herself. It was always a time for sharing thoughts and worries and secrets, enjoying being together without continual interruptions from the rest of the family.

But today Mrs. Morley moved up the hill against the wind tight-lipped and silent, wrapped up in her own thoughts. She even walked a few feet ahead of Lynn, as though she hardly even realized that her daughter was along. It made Lynn feel terribly lonely and left out.

Just before they reached Mrs. Tuggle's gate, however, Mrs. Morley stopped and knelt over something there in the grass.

"Look, Lynn," she said, and her voice again had the soft sound it used to have. "Daffodils. In a few more weeks they'll be in bloom." She slipped one arm around Lynn and pointed out the green stems growing in the shade of some bushes.

Lynn leaned against her mother and wished she could make the moment last. It was as though Mother was slipping away from all of them, and no one quite knew what to do to bring her back.

They knocked at the big oak door, and Lynn stared hard at the troll door knocker. Then she blinked. The eyes *did* move. She was sure of it. This time, instead of backing away, Lynn stepped forward and stared hard at the knocker. Then she discovered that the metal eyes of the creature had small holes in the centers so that someone standing on the other side of the door could look out. Mrs. Tuggle had been watching.

The door opened. Mrs. Tuggle smiled at Mother, but she did not smile at Lynn.

"I've brought a helper today, Mrs. Tuggle," Mother explained. "It's certainly a nice morning, isn't it?"

"Aye, not as cold as it was yesterday," the old woman said.

Lynn followed her mother up the stairs, but she had the uneasy feeling that Mrs. Tuggle was staring after her. When they reached the top, she paused for a moment and looked back. Mrs. Tuggle was standing at the bottom, and her face was terrible. Her eyes, like two simmering coals, blazed out at Lynn under her heavy black eyebrows, and she looked like an animal ready to spring.

Lynn hurried on after her mother and closed the upstairs door behind them.

She had scarcely settled herself in one corner of the room with Mother's loose-leaf binder on her lap than there was a light tap at the door, and Mrs. Tuggle came in carrying a pot of tea and two cups.

"Ah! My morning tea!" Mrs. Morley said, putting down her pen and smiling. "See how she pampers me, Lynn?"

"There's nothing like a spot of hot tea on a cold morning to warm the fingers," said the old woman, setting the tray down on the corner of Mother's desk. She sounded, Lynn decided, like the witch in Hansel and Gretel, fattening up Hansel and checking his fingers each morning.

Lynn said nothing. She watched Mrs. Tuggle go out again, but noticed that the door did not close all the way. She could just make out Mrs. Tuggle's eyes through the crack. For several moments the eyes kept their silent watch. Then finally they disappeared, and Lynn could hear the old woman's footsteps retreating down the stairs. She shivered.

"Want some tea, Lynn?" Mrs. Morley asked, pouring a cup for herself.

"No," Lynn said. "I don't need anything."

As the morning wore on, however, Lynn realized that her mother's writing seemed to be going slower and slower. When Mrs. Morley first sat down at the desk, she had seemed perky and energetic and eager to get to her manuscript. By ten o'clock, however, she sat leaning back in her chair, holding the cup in her hands, letting the strange fragrant mist bathe her face. Only occasionally then did she pick up her pen, and when she wrote at all, her eyes seemed to be half closed.

The tea! thought Lynn. That was it! Hadn't Mother mentioned once that even when she worked in her studio outside, Mrs. Tuggle brought her tea sometimes? Now she was drinking it every day. There was something about that tea. . . .

Lynn continued her cutting and arranging and pasting of the clippings in the notebook, but her mind was rushing on ahead, tumbling over ideas. Perhaps this was how Mrs. Tuggle was gaining control of her mother. Perhaps it was the tea that was making Mother brooding and distant. Why hadn't Lynn thought of this before?

Memories came rushing back. Each time, during the past year, that she and Marjorie had come to visit the old woman, Mrs. Tuggle had gone right to the kitchen and boiled the water for tea. Even when they politely declined it, she tried to persuade them to drink it anyway. And once, after drinking a full cup, Mouse had seemed to fall into a spell.

'Tis my own special brew, Mrs. Tuggle had told them once, *made of branch water*. She told them that she collected the herbs herself from the woods and meadows, and used the water in Cowden's Creek, which she boiled in the old pot on her stove.

"I think I'll have some of that tea after all," Lynn said suddenly, going over to the tray and pouring some in the second cup.

"It won't be very hot," Mother commented.

"That's okay."

Lynn sat down with the tea. It was barely warm. She sipped it slowly, feeling nothing. Perhaps the tea had to be hot to have an effect. Perhaps it was the mist and the steam swirling into the facial pores that made the eyelids heavy and the lower lip seem to sag, giving the impression, almost, that the drinker had been drugged.

Lynn put down the cup and concentrated on her work again. She was trimming an old yellowed clipping that Mother had cut out of a newspaper several years ago and stuffed in her witchcraft folder. "Charm Believed Responsible for Man's Death," it said, and Lynn glanced at it as she prepared it for the notebook. Then she stopped suddenly and read it again. It told about a man in Britain who jumped to his death from a cliff into the sea. His sister blamed a charm that he was wearing about his neck, which she said a witch had once given to him. The sister went on to say that she had heard that when a person wore an evil charm, a part of himself would fall under the spell of the witches, and they could command the person to do things that ordinarily he would not.

Lynn thought again of the charm the cat had worn about its neck. What if Judith discovered it, put it on, and found herself in Mrs. Tuggle's control after her long ordeal the previous summer? What if little Stevie, playing detective, found the charm and put it around his neck? Lynn shuddered. She would have to hide it in a better place.

And then Lynn realized that the tea was having an effect after all. The scissors slid off her lap onto the floor, and as she reached for them, she felt just a little dizzy. She was reacting more slowly than usual, she discovered. She felt sleepy, as though, in an unguarded moment, her eyelids would close of their own accord. So this was what had been happening with Mother.

It took all the energy Lynn could muster to finish the page she was working on. At noon, Mother got out their sandwiches and they sat nibbling them quietly. Lynn had hoped that at lunch they could relax and talk to each other, but Mrs. Tuggle appeared with a new pot of tea, and Mother poured herself another cup and sat over it in silence.

Lynn drank no more. By one o'clock, she was beginning to feel a little more like herself, more awake.

But during this time her mind had been clear enough to come to a decision: she would find some way to steal down to Mrs. Tuggle's kitchen and take away her supply of tea.

She had gone down the hall to use the bathroom, and was just coming back when she heard the sound of the heavy knocker on the front door. She stood very still in the shadows at the top of the stairs and listened. She heard Mrs. Tuggle's footsteps on the floor below and the slow creak of the big door. Finally a man's voice filled the entrance hall:

"Mrs. Elnora Tuggle?"

"Yes . . ."

"Good afternoon. I'm Mr. Sims from the County Sheriff's office, and we've been asked by the folks at the courthouse to help bring some of their records up to date."

Mrs. Tuggle did not reply, so the man went on:

"I believe you have a relative buried at the old cemetery."

"Two of them. My brother and my husband."

"Yes, that's what we were told. But it seems that the death certificate for your brother is missing, and I've got to ask you some questions to help us locate it. Would you mind if I stepped in for a few minutes? It's all routine, you understand."

"Of course. Do come in and have some tea."

"Oh, no, thank you, Ma'am. Never touch it." Mr. Sims laughed a little. "But you go right ahead and make yourself a cup. Still pretty cold outside."

The voices grew softer as Mrs. Tuggle and her visitor went into the parlor, and then Lynn could hear Mrs. Tuggle's footsteps in the kitchen where she was putting the kettle on to boil.

This was her chance. She would wait until she heard voices in the parlor again. Mrs. Tuggle would be talking with the man at least ten minutes. She would slip down to the kitchen and take the whole supply of tea.

She returned to the room where Mother was working. This time Mrs. Morley had her head down in her arms on the desk, as though she had fallen asleep. Perfect. Absolutely perfect. She moved out into the hall again, waiting.

Finally she heard the sound of voices again in the parlor and the clink of Mrs. Tuggle's teacup on her saucer. The interview had begun.

Stealthily she made her way down the stairs, a step at a time. Just before she reached the bottom where she would be seen through the doorway to the parlor, she climbed over the stair railing and let herself slowly down on the other side. A moment later she was standing in the dark kitchen, and the cupboards loomed high above her.

Somehow Lynn had thought that when she walked in the kitchen she would find four cannisters on the counter labeled "flour," "sugar," "coffee," and "tea," and that all she would have to do would be to empty out the tea into a paper bag and leave.

The high, dark counter, however, did not at all resemble Mother's kitchen at home, with things neatly labeled and a large space left bare for Mrs. Morley to do her kneading and rolling and cutting.

There was only one window in the Tuggle kitchen besides the one in the back door and it was high up in the wall, as though purposely designed to prevent people from looking in. And because little sunlight fell in the room, the corners were dark and the cupboards themselves cast shadows on the counter below, which was cluttered with crocks and bowls and tall, vinegary-looking bottles which gave no clue at all as to where the tea was kept.

From down the dark hallway, there was a pause in the conversation, and Lynn stopped in her tracks, her heart beating faster. Then the voices began again:

". . . you have no copy of the death certificate your-self, Mrs. Tuggle?"

"Sure I am it's somewhere, but I'm an old woman, Mr. Sims, and 'twas a long time ago I lost my brother. Things pile up in an old lady's house, you know. Why, I've boxes in my attic and trunks in the cellar and drawers full of old papers. . . ."

Lynn crept quietly over to the cupboard nearest the stove. This was certainly the most logical place for her to look. Mrs. Tuggle drank tea so often that she would probably keep it close to the kettle on the stove. She reached up and softly opened the cupboard door, pausing to see if the slight click of the latch had inter-rupted the conversation in the front room, but the voices continued:

"It would be a great help to us, Mrs. Tuggle, if you would look through your papers at your earliest convenience and see if perhaps you could find a copy of the death certificate. Then we could make a duplicate of it for our files, and would not have to trouble you about it again."

"There are a half dozen trunks, Mr. Sims," Mrs. Tuggle told him, "and more boxes than I can count. Old ladies are collectors, you know. 'Twould take me several years to go through it all."

"Perhaps I could arrange to have some clerks from the office help you."

Mrs. Tuggle's laugh was soft and harsh at the same time. Lynn, listening from the kitchen, wondered if the man from the sheriff's office realized that it had taken on a different quality.

" 'Twould not be that easy to find. 'Tis likely I've tucked it in a letter somewhere—a personal letter, you know. I don't think I would want your clerks opening my personal letters. . . ."

"They wouldn't read them, of course, Mrs. Tuggle."

"No, 'tis best done by me. Perhaps when the weather is warmer and the attic is not so cold. . . ."

There was nothing on the shelf that looked like tea to Lynn. There were several jars of jelly and a few cans of spice. There was a tall crock of pickles and some mustard and a can of cocoa. Softly, she closed the door and opened another. Dishes. Nothing but cups and saucers and dessert plates. Her elbow banged the door as she was withdrawing her hand and made a dull thud.

She stood rooted to the floor, her mouth open so that even her breathing was stilled.

For what seemed a stretch of twenty or thirty seconds, there was no sound at all from the living room. Finally, however, the squeak of Mrs. Tuggle's rocking chair began again, and Lynn heard Mr. Sims say:

"In case we don't ever find that certificate, Mrs. Tuggle, would you please describe for me as accurately as possible the circumstances of your brother's death? I know it was a long time ago. . . ."

". . . and the memory of an old woman is no longer sharp," Mrs. Tuggle added.

"Of course. I understand. But it would be helpful to us if we could have your account for our records, so that if there is ever a question. . . ."

"A question, Mr. Sims? What is there to ask about a fine young lad carried off by the flood when he was a mere sixteen? Seems enough sadness to last forever without stirring it up again after so many years."

"Believe me, Mrs. Tuggle, I can understand how hard this must be for you, and we've no wish to subject you to an unnecessary ordeal. But you must understand our position also. There cannot help but be questions when it has been discovered that only one death certificate out of all of those buried in the old cemetery is missing. . . ."

"Then the questions should go to the courthouse, not to me, young man. 'Tis not me who misfiled it."

"Of course not. But it's important for us to establish that there was, indeed, a death certificate made out for your brother. Can you tell me how long after he was discovered missing that the body was found?"

"Two days, Mr. Sims. Early of the morning. For two days we searched, and then my husband found the body caught in the weeds and the rocks beneath the old footbridge—or where the footbridge was, because sure the bridge was under water, so deep the creek ran that spring."

"And then what, Mrs. Tuggle?"

"Then we buried him, of course."

"But did no one else see him? No doctor?"

"Why should we have called a doctor, Mr. Sims? The lad was dead."

"But surely you reported it. Surely the county sent someone out . . . the coroner. . . ."

"I am sure that my husband did whatever needed to be done," Mrs. Tuggle said tersely. "As for me, the grief was so deep that I do not really remember. . . ."

Lynn had been so entranced with the conversation that she had momentarily forgotten the tea. She stood there by the cupboard listening, straining to hear.

"My husband made the coffin himself," Mrs. Tuggle's voice went on. "Oak, it was. I remember. And we buried him there in the old cemetery."

"Was there a funeral?"

"We did not have many friends in those days, Mr. Sims. But of course we told the neighbors."

"And the gravestone? What about that?"

"We ordered it and put it on a year later. A pretty penny it cost us, too, but I wanted the boy to have a gravestone like none other, and there he rests."

➤ Lynn knew she would have to hurry if she were to
find the tea before the conversation ended. She moved
quickly to the next cupboard in the corner and opened
the door. This cupboard was even darker, and full of
little cloth bags. She quickly picked up the first little
bag and peered inside. Cornmeal. She put it back and
tried a second. Raisins. She reached for a sack near the
back and squeezed it, feeling for the dry crunch of
leaves that would mean tea. Suddenly:

"What are you doing in my kitchen?"

Mrs. Tuggle seemed to have appeared from nowhere, and grabbed Lynn's arm so tightly that Lynn gave a little cry. The old woman's fingers felt icy cold, like the touch of death itself.

Lynn's first impulse was to scream. At least it would signal someone that she was in trouble. Then she heard the front door close and knew that Mr. Sims had left. Still, Mother was upstairs. Mrs. Tuggle dared not hurt her with Mother in the house. But suddenly she thought of a better answer than a scream.

"We wanted some more tea," she said, and tried to sound as polite and convincing as she could under the circumstances. "I saw that you had a visitor and didn't want to interrupt you. But I couldn't find the tea."

Mrs. Tuggle's fingers relaxed and her eyes showed a trace of pleased surprise. "More tea your mother wants, eh? Well, I shall fix up a pot and take it to her." She reached back into a dark shelf, one that Lynn had not yet searched, and brought down a small tin of tea, then reached under the stove and pulled out a burlap sack.

"Go on," she said suddenly to Lynn. " 'Twill take awhile to brew. I'll bring it up myself when it's ready."

Lynn walked slowly upstairs, thinking. The can of tea looked like any that she could buy at the store. There was nothing at all unusual about it. But the burlap sack . . . something had been sticking out the top . . . something familiar. What was it? And then she remembered a certain plant that grew along the bank by Mrs. Tuggle's portion of the creek. The stems had obviously been picked in the fall when they were dry and had tassled. It must be that the old woman grew it and used it to mix with other tea. "My own special brew," she used to say. Of course. That was it. It was not the tea at all, but what she added to it!

Mother was still resting with her head in her arms. She did not seem to have moved at all. Lynn was beginning to feel worried.

"Mother?" she said, lightly shaking her arm. "Mother, are you okay?"

Mrs. Morley sat up slowly, looking groggily about, and covered her face with her hands.

"I'm so sleepy!" she said. "Is it too warm up here, or is it just me?"

"It is sort of warm," Lynn said. "I'll turn off the radiator for you and see if that helps."

Mother yawned. "Thanks, dear. How's the work coming?"

"I've finished a whole folder. I think I'll go to Marjorie's now if you don't mind."

"Of course not. Go ahead." Mother sat up and picked up the papers in front of her to look them over. "I wonder if I will ever finish the last chapter. I thought that being up here in Mrs. Tuggle's house would help— the atmosphere, the gloom . . . put me in the right frame of mind. But it seems to be taking forever. I keep falling asleep. And if *I* keep going to sleep, what can I expect from my readers?"

Lynn was about to answer that she didn't think it was the writing that was putting Mother to sleep but rather the tea, or what was in it, but at that moment footsteps sounded in the hall, and Mrs. Tuggle came in.

As soon as she entered, her back to Lynn, Lynn picked up her coat and stole quickly through the doorway and down the stairs to the kitchen. Noiselessly she opened the cupboard beneath the stove, grabbed the big burlap sack of herbs, thrust it under her coat, and went out the front door just as she heard Mrs. Tuggle's feet on the stairs again.

She ran as though all the fiends of hell were behind her, her coat lumpy and huge from the bag beneath it. She did not stop running until she was halfway down the block. Then she slowed to a fast walk and thrust her nose down under her coat to sniff at the bag. That was it! That was the smell exactly!

She knocked at the Beasley door and waited. Mouse was eating a peanut butter and onion sandwich. She was the only person Lynn had ever known who carefully spread her bread with butter, then with peanut butter, and then thin transparent slices of Bermuda onion. It had to be Bermuda, Mouse always said. Lynn could smell what she was eating even before she saw the peanut butter.

"What's this?" Mouse asked, looking at the sack.

"We're going to have a tea party," Lynn said. "Tea, as in Boston."

"What? What are you talking about?"

"We're about to have a Boston tea party, Mouse. I want you to come with me and dump this sack in the creek."

"Where did you get it?"

"It's Mrs. Tuggle's entire supply of whatever it is she's been putting in her tea . . . I hope."

Marjorie's eyes grew huge and her mouth dropped open, showing the peanut butter on her teeth.

"You're *kidding!*"

"See for yourself." Lynn opened the bag.

"It's just a mess of weeds!" Mouse said.

"Not weeds, exactly. It's an herb of some sort, and it only grows along Mrs. Tuggle's part of the creek. She planted them there, I'm sure of it. She crumbles up the tassles, I'll bet, and brews them along with tea from the store."

Marjorie stood staring quizzically down into the bag. "But why do you want to get rid of it, Lynn? It will only make her furious. She's English, you know. She can't live without tea."

"Maybe not, but she can live without this stuff in it. And Mom will live a lot *better* without it. Mouse, I'm sure that this is pulling Mother into Mrs. Tuggle's power. Do you remember last summer when Mrs. Tuggle gave us some tea, and you almost fell asleep, just like Mother's doing? It must have some kind of narcotic effect. It makes us more suggestible, more easy to manipulate."

"But Lynn, when she discovers that the sack is gone, she'll just go down and get some more."

"She has to wait till the plant tassles again, Mouse. See? This is the part she uses . . ." Lynn crumbled some up in her hand. "They won't tassle again till fall."

"She'll be livid. She'll hate us forever."

"She already does, Mouse."

"Oh, Lynn, it just won't work! She'll just find another way to control your mother! If she can't make tea, she'll mix up some other potion and call it something else. She's probably working on it right now."

"It's a chance we'll have to take, Mouse. Come on. I almost expect her to come running down here after us."

It was starting to rain. The air was decidedly warmer now than it had been for some time. Soon the spring rains would begin and then the peach trees would bloom, and after that the honeysuckle would flood the air with its fragrant smell. As the girls started across the Beasley back yard and to the creek beyond, Lynn felt a special longing for summer—for an end to the cold and the gloom and the fear that wouldn't seem to let go.

She wanted to spend her summers sitting lazily on the back porch glider with Mouse, singing a duet or planning a slumber party or making chocolate chip cookies with Stevie. She wished that Mrs. Tuggle would just disintegrate, she decided as they reached the creek and dumped the contents of the sack in the water. She wished that the old woman would just float away as the stalks of the plant were doing, their tassles caught in the current, twisting and whirling, and then rushing on down the hill toward the business district. She and Mouse stood there silently and watched them go.

"Lynn Morley, what on earth have you done?"

Lynn whirled around. There was Mother striding

across the field, her face wet with the rain, and the scarf—which held back her hair from her face—hanging bedraggled over one shoulder.

Lynn could not think of a reply.

"Mother, you're soaking wet!" was all she could say.

"And so are you, young lady. What is this all about?"

"What is what all about?" Lynn asked feebly as Mouse shrank back.

"This!" Mrs. Morley pointed to the empty bag. "What have you done with Mrs. Tuggle's tea? As soon as you left her house, she came upstairs and said she suspected you had stolen her tea. I couldn't imagine such a thing! I called home but Judith said you weren't there, so I knew you were with Marjorie."

Mrs. Morley's eyes, angry and unsympathetic, darted back and forth from Lynn to Mouse.

"I dumped it in the creek," Lynn said.

"You *what?*" Mrs. Morley stared at her. "Do you realize that is her entire supply of tea?"

Inside, Lynn felt jubilant. She was afraid that perhaps the old woman had bushels of it left in her cellar.

"No," she said to her mother. "She has plenty of tea. It's this plant, this drug, that she's out of now, Mother, and she's been putting it in your tea every day to get control of your mind."

Mother angrily snatched the sack away from Lynn. "That's nonsense! Utter nonsense! I'm upset and angry with you, Lynn Morley!"

"Mother, please believe me! You know how sleepy you've been feeling! You know how difficult it's been

95

for you to finish that chapter! I'm trying to save you before it's too late."

"Go home, Lynn," her mother said coldly. "I will never invite you to Mrs. Tuggle's house with me again."

chapter six

It was strange and silent in the Morley house that night.
Mother was still angry—hurt and angry—and Lynn
knew that she would tell Father what she had done.
She did not think that Mother would tell him at the
dinner table, however. It was just understood that when
someone was scolded, it was not to be in front of the
whole family. But on this particular evening, the rule
was broken.

"Lynn did a terrible thing today," Mother said, setting the stew pot down in the center of the table.

Judith looked across the table at her sister and Lynn
felt her face grow hot.

"What did she do?" Stevie asked curiously, staring.

Father, too, looked quizzical.

"Do we have to talk about it now?" he asked.

But Mother ignored the question.

"She stole something from Mrs. Tuggle."

Lynn knew that no one in the family ever expected something like this. That she might be careless and break something valuable, they would believe. That she and Mouse had been acting silly and done something embarrassing, or that Lynn might have a quarrel with Judith or even slap Stevie, Father would believe. But who would ever think that she could coldly, calculatingly, steal something?

Father sat without moving.

"What did she take, Sylvia?"

"Mrs. Tuggle's entire supply of tea. A huge burlap bag of it."

"Tea!" exclaimed Judith.

"Wow!" Stevie gasped. "She sure must like tea!"

Father slowly pulled the stew pot toward him and ladled some out into his dish.

"That true, Lynn?" he asked.

"No," said Lynn.

The heavy spoon clunked in the pot. Father looked at her. "It's not?"

"I did not take her tea," Lynn said precisely. "I took a sack of dried plants that she has been brewing along with her tea."

Father looked at Lynn for a long time. He started to ask her something, then changed his mind. "What did you do with it?"

"I threw it in the creek."

"It may be just a sack of herbs to you, Lynn, but to Mrs. Tuggle it's a necessary ingredient in her own special brew, and she misses it terribly," Mother said. "She says she won't be able to get any more till next fall when the plant tassles again. Naturally, she is very upset, and I am shocked that our daughter would do something so awful."

"I'm surprised," Father said at last, "but I can't help but feel that if Lynn did something like that she must have had a reason. And I would rather wait till later, if you don't mind, to find out what the reason was."

Lynn could not believe her own ears. She simply could not believe it. All these months it had been Father more than anyone else who scoffed at Lynn's fears about Mrs. Tuggle and witchcraft. Lynn had suspected that tonight he would be furious and out of patience with her. But he was not.

The meal continued in silence. Dinner times at the Morley house were usually festive affairs—the gathering of everybody around the table, each telling of funny or unusual or interesting things that had happened that day. But when there was tension between Mr. and Mrs. Morley, the others sensed it, and the table fell silent.

Lynn sat on her side of the table beside Stevie, eating her lima beans one by one, stabbing each with the prongs of her fork, making four neat holes across the broad green belly of each bean, then turning her fork the other way and making another row of holes in the other direction, like an "X" on each bean. The witch's mark, she thought. Was that how Mrs. Tuggle worked

her magic, by thinking witchy thoughts as she performed her rituals, projecting all her strength into the thing she wished to have happen until finally it did? Did she have something to do with Mr. and Mrs. Beasley's getting a divorce, perhaps, and was she working it now on Mother and Father?

Once, when Lynn had asked her mother whether she and Father would ever separate, Mother had laughed and said, "It would be a lie to tell you that it was impossible, Lynn, because few things are really impossible. But it certainly seems improbable. We get along quite well together, I think. The problem is that we get

along *so* well, that you rarely hear us quarrel. And when
we do have a tiff, or we're not saying much to each
other, it seems so unusual that it makes you upset."
Lynn wondered whether that was true now.

"Quit fooling around with your food, Lynn." Mother's voice sounded sharp and unfriendly.

Lynn speared four lima beans at once and put them
in her mouth, then excused herself and went up to her
room.

She had just sat down on the edge of the bed when
Stevie came in.

"What do you want?" Lynn asked impatiently, and

then wondered about the tone of her own voice. This is what happened when there was tension in the family. First the tension was between her and Mother, then Mother and Father, now her and Stevie. Anger was contagious.

"What do you want, Stevie?" she asked again, more gently.

- In answer, Stevie just sat down on the round rug in the center of the floor and looked at her. It was as though he didn't want to get too close, Lynn thought, as though he didn't really quite trust her. It hurt.

"I'm supposed to ask you where the chain is—the one the cat wore," he said finally.

Lynn stared at him.

"Who told you to ask me?"

"Mrs. Tuggle."

"Why does she think that I have it?"

"She just does. I saw her out walking yesterday and she said she has a feeling that the cat's chain is in our house someplace, and that I should ask you where it is. If I find it for her, she's going to give me a dollar and fifty cents."

So the price was going up. Mrs. Tuggle wanted it back very badly.

"Do you think that I have it, Stevie?" Lynn stalled.

"Yes. Because you took her tea. I'll bet you took the cat, too."

"Stevie, where on earth would I keep her cat?"

"I don't know, but I'll bet you've got its chain. Boy, I'll bet you've stole lots of stuff, Lynn! That's why

Mommy's so mad at you."

Lynn slid off the bed and sat down on the rug beside Stevie. She was glad that he didn't shrink away from her. He still *wanted* to trust. . . .

"Stevie," she said. "If I told you that I'm afraid Mrs. Tuggle might hurt Mother, and that I stole the tea to protect her, would you feel better about me?"

Stevie looked at Lynn. "You don't like Mrs. Tuggle, do you?"

Lynn pressed her lips together. "I'm afraid of her, Stevie—afraid of what she's doing to Mother—of what she could do to all of us. There are lots of questions that need to be answered about Mrs. Tuggle, and until we have the answers, it would be a good idea if you just stayed away from her completely."

She had left her school books down in the music room, Lynn discovered later, after Stevie had gone to his own room to play. She went downstairs to the second floor and then started down to first, but when she reached the turn at the landing, she heard her parents' voices in the kitchen, and stopped.

". . . just let her get away with something like that," Mother was saying. "She *stole* that tea, Richard, like a common ordinary thief, and all you can say is, 'She must have had a reason.' Have you lost your senses? What kind of an example is that for Stevie? How on earth can we justify her walking right in that woman's kitchen and taking something from the cupboard? And then to *destroy* it! She can't even be made to give it back!"

"I'll talk to her," Father said. "But meanwhile, Sylvia, I'm concerned about you."

"That's ridiculous."

"No, it's not. It seems ridiculous because you think you can take care of yourself. But I'm as worried about you as you were about Judith last summer. You were uneasy then about her relationship with Mrs. Tuggle, and wondered if Lynn's suspicions might be right. Well, now I'm worried about you."

"Oh, Richard, you can't possibly believe all that nonsense!"

"All I know for sure is that something is happening to you, and I can see it better than you can. You haven't been yourself. Sometimes you act completely normal, and other times you're unreachable. I can't help but think that Lynn took the tea because she's worried too."

"Of course that's why she took it, but it's positively ridiculous! She says that Mrs. Tuggle's drugging the tea or something, and that the weeds or herbs or whatever is the culprit. Richard, that child needs to see a psychologist."

"Maybe. But what if she's right?"

There was a pause, and Lynn's heart pounded.

"Well! I never thought I'd hear you say that!" came Mother's voice.

"I just said that maybe Lynn's right in being concerned about you and your relationship with Mrs. Tuggle. I'm not prepared to claim more than that."

There was the noise of the refrigerator door closing

as Mother put things away. "You sound as though you suspect something."

"I don't know what to think. Bob Sims, from the sheriff's office, went up to see Mrs. Tuggle this afternoon about that missing death certificate. He talked with me about it later. He asked her if she had a copy of it. At first she acted as though she were sure there was one somewhere, but made it sound as though it would be impossible to find it in all her trunks. She also rejected his offer to send someone over to help her look for it."

"That doesn't surprise me too much. You know how old women misplace things, and that was a long time ago. She's always lived off to herself, so naturally she wouldn't want somebody going through her things."

"Yes, I agree. But when Bob asked her the details of the death and the burial, it looks more and more as though the Tuggles buried the boy without anyone else knowing about it. She says they didn't call a doctor because he was already dead, and as for calling the coroner, she can't remember whether they did or not."

"But surely a young boy couldn't just disappear suddenly without anyone asking questions, Richard. . . ."

"That's what I keep telling myself, but it happened at the time of the big flood. The whole business district was under water. Four people lost their lives that spring, and everyone was concerned with his own problems. Houses were washed away, basements were flooded. It could have been several weeks before Mrs. Tuggle told the neighbors that her brother had drowned, and everyone could have assumed that there had been a quiet family funeral. After all, the Tuggles never did mix much. Lived off to themselves in the house at the top of the hill. . . ."

"Then perhaps that's exactly what happened. Perhaps they didn't think it was necessary to have a coroner."

"Maybe. But it's also possible that they didn't *want* anyone to see his body, to know that the death wasn't accidental."

"Okay, Dick. Say it out loud. The suspicion is that Mrs. Tuggle killed her own brother and that her husband helped cover up for it. Right? Is that what everyone's saying? Is that what you believe, too?"

"That's what people are saying, yes. I don't know what to believe yet. All I know, Sylvia, is that the kids and I are worried about you. You haven't been yourself, especially since you moved your studio into Mrs. Tuggle's house for the winter. If Lynn suspects that Mrs. Tuggle is putting something in your tea that makes you act this way, then she stole that bag of stuff because she loves you. And that's exactly how I feel. How can I scold her for that?"

"Oh, Dick, I guess I have been too hard on her. And I guess I have seemed distracted. But it annoys me no end that everyone attributes it to that poor old woman, when it's simply that I'm having a terrible time on the last chapter. I think about it constantly and I can't seem to end it properly."

"Then meet us halfway," Father said. "Bring your

writing things home and finish the book here. Then we won't be worrying about you, and we'll let the sheriff's office concern itself with Mrs. Tuggle."

"I only have a few more pages to go," Mother said. "I should finish it in a week, and then I'll come back here and work till the weather's warmer. I promise."

"I'd rather you finished the book here," Father said.

"Now that's just too silly. A few more days won't hurt. You see, I want to be able to tell my editor that the book was written in an upstairs room of a creaky old house on a hill so she can put it in the blurb on the dust jacket. And it would hardly be accurate if, in fact, I finished it here at home."

"It won't be accurate anyway," argued Father. "You wrote over half the book in a remodeled henhouse."

"I know, but the last chapter is so climactic, and I just feel I think better if I'm sitting in that upstairs room with the shadows all around and the floor creaking and Mrs. Tuggle gliding in and out like a ghost. . . ."

Lynn got her books from the music room. She heard her mother going downstairs to the cellar to put some jars away. When she turned to go back up to her room, she saw her father standing in the kitchen doorway.

"Lynn," he said. "I don't want you to go to Mrs. Tuggle's house again. I want you to promise me that."

Lynn stopped. She looked straight in her father's eyes.

"I can't," she said, but her voice was almost inaudible.

Father's voice, too, was gentle. "Why can't you?"

"Because I may not be able to keep it."

"Why not?"

"Because . . . because somebody has to look out for Mom," Lynn said. "When Mother stops going to Mrs. Tuggle's house, I won't go there either."

Father watched her thoughtfully. Lynn could not tell if he was displeased or not. "All right," he said finally. "When Mother stops going, then. . . ."

Lynn went back up to her room with her school books, and she felt both incredibly strong and brave. Father trusted her. He might not believe everything she believed about Mrs. Tuggle, but he trusted her. Perhaps he realized that someone would have to keep an eye on Mother next week.

She had just spread out her history books on her bed and was starting a paper on Alexander Hamilton when Judith came upstairs.

"Did Dad talk to you yet?" she asked, coming over.

"Yes."

"What did he say? Did he bawl you out?"

"No."

"He didn't? You mean you walked right into Mrs. Tuggle's house and stole something, and you're not even going to be punished? Lynn, whatever got into you? What would make you do a thing like that? I swear, this whole household is going nuts!"

How much should she tell her, Lynn wondered. How much did she dare? It was Judith they had been worried about once. If Lynn told her everything she knew about the old woman, would Judith slip under Mrs. Tuggle's power again? Would she become afraid and restless and uneasy? Was it better, perhaps, to let her go on forgetting whatever it was that had happened to her up there in the house on the hill?

But Mother was in danger, and perhaps it was time for risk-taking.

"Sit down, Judith," Lynn said at last. "I've got something to tell you."

"I have the feeling that things are going on I don't know anything about," Judith said. "Dad seems worried about Mom. You're doing crazy things. . . ."

"Judith," said Lynn, and she chose her words carefully. It felt rather strange to be talking to her older sister like this. "When you were going to Mrs. Tuggle's to sew last spring and summer, did you know that we were worried about you? At least I was. And Mother too, I think, though she tried not to show it."

"Worried about me? Why?"

"Because you were acting strangely—sort of like Mother has been acting lately. And then you got very sick. Do you remember any of that?"

Judith frowned thoughtfully. "I remember being sick. At least, I remember getting well, and everybody told me I'd had mononucleosis. I hardly remember anything at all about being at Mrs. Tuggle's house, though. That's strange, isn't it, because it was less than a year ago."

"I never wanted to remind you of it," Lynn went on.

"I guess I've always been afraid that if you remembered, Mrs. Tuggle's power over you would begin all over again."

Judith sat staring at Lynn. For a long, long time she did not say anything at all, and Lynn decided that it was better not to go into too much detail.

"You really do believe that Mrs. Tuggle is a witch, don't you, Lynn? It isn't just some silly game that you and Mouse are playing."

"No, it's not."

"I guess down deep I *have* known that something went on up there in her house that wasn't good for me, but I don't remember what, and I haven't wanted to talk about it, because . . . well, just thinking about it makes me uncomfortable. I don't know why. But why would Mrs. Tuggle be working her witchcraft on Mother, of all people?"

"I'm not sure. I think it has something to do with the old cemetery. For some reason she doesn't want her brother's grave disturbed, and maybe she thinks Mother can help her stop the city from doing it."

"Does Dad believe this?"

"I don't know. He believes that Mrs. Tuggle is having a bad effect on Mother somehow, but I don't know how much he believes in witchcraft."

"But what can we do?"

"I don't know. We certainly can't stop her from going up there every day."

Judith thought it over. "I could get real sick again. I could go into convulsions and everything, and make her stay here and take care of me."

"That wouldn't work, Judith, and you know it. She'd take your temperature right away and know you were faking. Besides, that would only put things off. She's determined to finish writing that chapter in Mrs. Tuggle's house. The sooner she finishes it and gets out of there, the better. We've got to protect her while she's there, that's all. That's why I stole the tea. If we just knew more about witchcraft! If we just knew how to fight whatever Mrs. Tuggle tries next!"

Again Judith was silent for a long time, and Lynn thought it best not to disturb her thoughts. But suddenly she sat straight up.

"Lynn, I've got it!"

"What?"

"Is Mouse still hypnotizing?"

"Yes, but why? You think she's going to hypnotize the secrets out of Mrs. Tuggle?"

"No. I want her to hypnotize me. I want her to ask me what I know about Mrs. Tuggle's secrets. It's worth a try."

"No, Judith!" Lynn was emphatic. "It's too dangerous. Mouse is only an amateur. It could start all kinds of things going on again for you. She could put you to sleep and not be able to wake you up or something. Your personality could change completely. Absolutely not!"

"Then I'm going to ask Marjorie myself."

"Judith, you shouldn't. I'll tell her not to."

"Listen, Lynn. If things are as serious as you think—

and they must be, because I've never seen Dad so worried—we've got to risk it. Mouse can ask me what you need to know, find out what Mrs. Tuggle did when I was there. And then she can tell me to forget everything again before I wake up. Maybe I won't be any help at all, but it's worth a try. You love Mom, don't you?"

"Of course I love Mom. That's a dumb question."

"Then you'll let Mouse hypnotize me."

Lynn took a deep breath. A dark sense of dread seemed to be overtaking her.

"No," she said. "Not unless we absolutely have to. We'll save that for last, Judith. But if it really comes to that, then I'll tell Mouse to go ahead."

Lynn slept fitfully that night. She was worried about her mother. She was worried about Judith. She was worried most of all because her father was worried, and she no longer had his calm reassurance, his kidding, his own disbelief, to keep her hoping that she and Mouse had been imagining things all along. Once she even got up in the night to be sure that Judith was still there, that she was all right. Then she fell asleep once more.

Mrs. Morley seemed more like herself at breakfast. She was unusually attentive to Lynn, as though making up for the previous evening. There was brown sugar for the oatmeal and special orange rolls that Lynn particularly liked. When Mother and Stevie set out together at eight-thirty—Mother for the house on the hill, and Stevie for kindergarten—Mrs. Morley kissed Lynn on the forehead.

"Have a good day, sweetheart," she said. "I think I'll make a Dutch apple pie for dinner. You like that, don't you?"

From the third floor window, Lynn saw Stevie running on ahead of Mother, pointing out tulips that were just coming up in a neighbor's yard, and Mother was walking briskly, eager, it seemed, to get to work and finish her book. Judith had already left for junior high school, and Lynn quickly pulled on her knee socks and sneakers, and looked out the window again to see if Mouse was coming up the hill.

As she tied her laces, she remembered Stevie's request that she tell him where the cat's chain had been hidden. The way he had looked at her, simply assuming that she had it. She was a thief, wasn't she? She decided to find a better hiding place for it than her dresser drawer. Perhaps she should bury it outside somewhere, or hide it under a pile of lumber in the basement.

She opened the top drawer of her dresser and reached down in the lefthand corner. Nothing.

Frantically she began throwing out socks and scarves, digging around for the chain, till the drawer was empty. The chain was gone.

She stood without moving in the center of the room. Last night, when she had gone downstairs for her school books, when she had stood there so long on the landing listening to her parents' conversation in the kitchen, Stevie must have slipped up to her room to look for the cat's chain. He had obviously found it and put it away for Mrs. Tuggle.

Lynn clattered downstairs to Stevie's room and rapidly searched his dresser drawers, his toy box, his closet, his shoes, even. Nothing. Where would a five-year-old hide something? She tried to think like Stevie, and checked his dump truck, his bank, his pillow, the box of blocks under the bed, but the chain wasn't there. And then she noticed that Stevie's window was half open and that the storm window beyond was unlocked. Her heart was in her mouth. Had Mrs. Tuggle somehow come in during the night, crept into Stevie's room, and taken the chain? Or was it possible that the old woman had come up to the third floor, even, and taken the chain while Lynn slept? Was that why Lynn had slept so fitfully? Why did Mrs. Tuggle want the chain so badly?

The constant ringing of the doorbell made her aware of the time, and she rushed downstairs, grabbed her coat, and bounded outside.

"I'm late," Mouse was saying. "I had to eat an egg for breakfast, and it took me ten minutes just to get it down."

"Mouse, I've got to catch Stevie before the bell rings," Lynn said, starting up the hill at a run.

"What's the matter?" Mouse asked, trying to catch up. Her glasses kept bobbing around on her nose and finally slid off altogether and hung by one ear.

"The cat's chain is gone," Lynn said numbly. "Stevie was asking me about it just last night. Mrs. Tuggle told him that I knew where it was. Someone took it out of my drawer, and I've got to know who."

chapter seven

They were a half block from the school when the first bell rang, and by the time they had reached the steps, the kindergarten children had been herded into the room at the far end of the hall.

"Tell Miss Collins I'll be late," Lynn told Mouse, and ran down the hall after Stevie.

The teacher had just seated the children on the floor for the morning show-and-tell when Lynn stepped into the room. Stevie smiled and waved and pointed her out to his friends.

"I'm Lynn Morley," Lynn told Stevie's teacher. "I need to talk with my brother for a minute. Could I take him out in the hall?"

"I guess you may," the teacher said. "Stevie, your

sister wants to speak to you."

Stevie got up wonderingly and followed Lynn out into the corridor.

"What is it?" he asked.

Lynn started to ask him what he had done with the cat's chain, and then realized that would be admitting that she had had it. So she said, "Did you go into my room last night when I wasn't there?"

Stevie rolled his tongue around in his mouth and squirmed uncomfortably.

"*Did* you?" Lynn demanded.

Stevie's guilty look turned defensive. "You had the cat's chain all the time!" he said accusingly. "You know you did! But it's not yours! It's Mrs. Tuggle's."

"What did you do with the chain, Stevie?"

"I'm not gonna tell you."

Lynn knelt down beside him. "Listen, Stevie. Please! Because Mother may need our help, and I can't help her unless I know who has the chain."

"Oh, Lynn, you just talk crazy. Mother doesn't need any help."

"She might, though, Stevie. Please tell me. I promise I won't get mad at you. Just tell me what you did with it."

"I dropped it out of my window."

"Why?"

"Mrs. Tuggle said if I ever found the chain I should just drop it out my window and she'd come by every morning to see if it was there and leave me a dollar and fifty cents under the azalea bush if it was. But I forgot to check this morning for my money. I don't know if she came or not."

Lynn stood up. "Thank you, Stevie," she said, trying hard to keep her promise about not being mad. "That's all I wanted to know."

She left her books outside her own classroom and ran all the way home as fast as she could. Her coat was unbuttoned and her hair was flying in the wind, but she didn't care. Perhaps it wasn't too late. Perhaps Mrs. Tuggle was waiting till after everyone had gone before she came snooping around the yard.

She reached home panting, completely out of breath, and made her way around the house to the place beneath Stevie's second floor window, holding her side with the pain of running. Desperately she searched the ground beneath the window. She got down on her hands and knees and examined every bush, every clump of grass. There was no chain. With sinking heart she walked over to the azalea bush in the corner of the yard. There, in a small brown box marked, "Stevie," was a fifty cent piece and four quarters.

At lunch time, Lynn and Mouse refused the other girls' offer to jump rope on the wide sidewalk in front of the school and sat, instead, on the railing along the parking lot where they could talk. The sun warmed their backs, but Lynn shivered anyway, and could not seem to stop the chill that traveled through her.

"If we just knew what she's going to do with it," Mouse said. "It's obviously terribly important to her, Lynn."

But Lynn didn't answer. She knew now that things had gone too far. Now it was time for risk-taking.

"Mouse," she said. "You've got to hypnotize Judith."

"Judith!"

"Yes. She asked me if you would. I told her last night about Mrs. Tuggle—about how it was when she was going there to sew. I didn't tell her everything, but she wants to help. She thinks that if you hypnotize her, she might remember something about Mrs. Tuggle that would be useful."

Mouse didn't answer for a moment. Her face looked flushed and pleased, as though she were a specialist being called upon to do something important. But there was a trace of panic in her eyes as well.

"What if I can't pull her out of it, Lynn? What if she turns into a witch right in front of our very eyes?"

"It's a chance we've got to take, Mouse. Judith says she's willing. Mother insists on writing at Mrs. Tuggle's for one more week. I'm so scared for her, Mouse. Anything could happen. If you were ever my friend, if you ever wanted to help me, now's the time to show it."

"I *am* your friend, Lynn, and I *do* want to help. But I'm scared spitless!"

"You can try, though."

"Yes, I'll try."

That afternoon, when Judith got off the bus at the bottom of the hill, Lynn and Marjorie were there waiting for her. They went directly to the Beasley home and up to Marjorie's bedroom.

Mouse pulled down the shades and lit a candle. She

propped Judith up on pillows against the headboard. Lynn decided to wait out in the hall so she wouldn't distract Judith. As she was about to leave the room, Judith caught her hand and stopped her.

"Lynn . . . just in case . . . I mean, if I never come out of it and they send me off to a loony house for the rest of my life, I want you to have all my jeans and my scrapbooks and records and stuff. . . ."

"Oh, lordie!" Mouse gasped, her voice quavery. She sat down shakily. "Don't talk that way, Judith. I'll be so scared I can't do it."

For an hour Mouse worked with Judith, but it seemed as though the session would not take. Mouse was nervous. The spoon she held in front of her dropped out of her hand once and clanked to the floor, snapping Judith's eyes wide open again. Judith herself lay tensely on the bed, her jaws in a determined set, trying hard to pay attention to Mouse and what she wanted her to do.

"You're trying too hard," Marjorie said at last. "You've got to relax, Judith. You've just got to pretend you're going to sleep. Let your mind wander. Go limp."

This time Mouse picked up the lighted candle and held it at the foot of the bed. She slowly moved her arm in a circle, so that the flame went round and round.

"You are sleepy, Judith," she said. "You are getting tired now of talking to me, and your eyes are getting heavy. You are no longer conscious of your arms and legs. The pillows are soft. You are sinking deeper and deeper down into the mattress. Sleep, Judith. Sleep."

Peeping around the corner, Lynn saw that Judith's eyelids were just dropping off to sleep.

"Your arms have no gravity, Judith," Mouse intoned, becoming more confident of herself. "Your right hand is light—as light as a feather—and it is going to rise slowly up in the air."

As Lynn watched, Judith's right hand slowly lifted from off the pillow where it had been resting and hung limply in the air like a snake.

"You are on your way to Mrs. Tuggle's with your sewing basket," Mouse went on. "You are going into the front door of her house, Judith, and now you are going up the stairs to the room on the second floor. Mrs. Tuggle is there waiting for you. Can you describe the room for us, Judith? Can you tell us what you see?"

Out in the hall, Lynn crouched on her knees and listened. Judith was speaking in a soft, faraway voice, as though she were barely awake.

"There are sewing things on the table . . . my skirt . . . my plaid skirt . . . and some cloth for a blouse . . . and scissors. . . ."

"Where is Mrs. Tuggle, Judith?"

"She is . . . she's sitting in the rocking chair in the corner."

"Is she sewing?"

Judith began to squirm a little. "No . . . it's not the night for sewing . . . it's the night for spell-making. I want to sew, but Mrs. Tuggle says I have to light the black candles. . . ."

Lynn got to her feet in the doorway and stood there

watching Mouse.

"W . . . what will happen when you light the black candles, Judith?" Mouse asked shakily.

At this question, Judith jerked her head to one side, agitated, and her body grew rigid. Lynn was alarmed.

"I don't know. I'm afraid," Judith said. "I'm afraid! I'm afraid!"

"Change the subject," Lynn whispered. "You're going too fast, Mouse. Ask her something else."

"What else is in the room, Judith?" Mouse inquired, looking desperately toward Lynn for help. "Is there anything really important? Anything secret?"

"Yes . . ." Judith sighed very deeply and grew quiet.

Lynn stepped inside the room, her eyes on her sister.

"What is in the room that is secret?" Mouse continued.

"A box," Judith answered softly.

"Where is the box?"

"On top the high bureau . . . up next to the ceiling."

"What is in the box, Judith?"

"I don't know. Something . . . that belonged to someone else . . . a long time ago. . . ."

Suddenly Judith's head began turning again and her fingers gripped the bedspread. "I must never tell anyone," she said, as if to herself. "I must go out of the room and never tell anyone. . . ."

At that moment there was the sound of a car door slamming outside in the driveway.

"Dad!" Mouse said in horror. "He's home!"

"Wake Judith," Lynn said, running over to the window as Mr. Beasley came up the walk.

Mouse rushed over to Judith and started to shake her, then stopped. "It's time to wake up, Judith," she said carefully. "When you open your eyes, you will not remember what we have talked about. You will feel strong, and you won't be afraid. When I clap my hands three times, you will open your eyes, but you won't remember our talk." Mouse then clapped her hands three times, loudly.

Judith rolled over on her side. Her eyelids fluttered, then closed, then fluttered again and finally opened.

"What time is it?" she asked sleepily.

Downstairs, there was the sound of the front door opening and closing, and then footsteps in the hall.

"Marjorie?" Mr. Beasley called.

"I'm up here," Mouse answered. "I've got some friends over."

"Okay. Just wondered if you were home."

Judith sat straight up. "What . . . what's happened? How come I'm over here?"

"You let Mouse hypnotize you," Lynn said.

Judith lay back against the pillow. "Did it work? Did I remember anything important?"

"Yes," said Lynn.

"What?"

"We can't tell you, Judith. It just wouldn't be good," Mouse said. "You'll have to trust us. We promised you would forget what we talked about."

"I guess I have," Judith said. "I just feel a little bit . . . oh, I don't know."

"What?" Lynn asked. "Try to tell us."

"A little bit scared, I guess. Like I *was* scared, but now it's over."

"That's good," said Mouse. "That's just the way it should be. But I'll never do this again, Lynn. That's the last time I'll ever hypnotize anyone. I've never been so scared in my life."

Judith got up and the three girls went downstairs, their faces pale. Lynn felt guilty for allowing it. What if Judith had not pulled through? A few questions more, the wrong questions, perhaps, and she might have simply gone berserk. She shivered and leaned against the wall as they moved down the stairs.

Mr. Beasley was standing in the hallway looking over the mail on the table, and Lynn wondered if he would realize how shaky they were.

"It's a note from Mrs. Tuggle," he said aloud, as if to himself. "She wants to know if she can come down to the store some time and look through all the books I bought from the Voight estate. I wonder why. She doesn't say. . . ."

Lynn and Mouse stared at each other. Mrs. Tuggle was obviously looking for the diary that Bertha Voight had kept, to see if she had said anything about her in it, anything that might give away information she would rather keep secret.

"Strange," Mr. Beasley said, and put the envelope back down. "People are beginning to say some pretty frightening things about that woman. I heard about the missing death certificate, Lynn. What does your father think about all this? What's the zoning commission decided to do with the old cemetery, anyway?"

"It hasn't decided," said Lynn. "They definitely want to move all the graves to the new cemetery on the east side, but they haven't decided whether to zone the old land for commercial property or what."

"Well, it would be a shame if they do," Mr. Beasley said emphatically. "I'm with Mrs. Tuggle on that. Some of those graves have been there a lot longer than we've been around. They've a right to stay. That's how I feel about it. There's enough steel and concrete in this town. I'll take trees any day."

The girls said a few polite words and went out on the porch.

"We've got a job to do tonight, Mouse," Lynn said.

Mouse nodded. She didn't need to be told what.

"What are you going to do?" Judith wanted to know.

"We can't tell you," Lynn replied. "The best thing you can do while we're gone, Judith, is keep a close eye on Mother and Stevie. Make sure nothing happens to either of them."

There was no Dutch apple pie for dinner. There was, in fact, almost no dinner at all. Mother had opened a can of mushroom soup and mixed it with chicken noodle. There was a jar of peanut butter on the table and a box of crackers. And Mrs. Morley herself sat by the window while the others ate, a faraway look in her eyes that frightened Lynn just to see it.

"Aren't you feeling well, Sylvia?" Father asked,

watching her from his end of the table. There was no reply.

Lynn and Judith looked at their father. Stevie was dropping pieces of crackers in his soup.

"I thought we were gonna have pie!" he said after a bit, trying to get a conversation going. "You said we were gonna have a pie, Mom!"

In answer, however, Mrs. Morley turned around and stared straight at Father.

"I think it's just terrible what they are doing to that poor woman!" she said. "Why are they hounding her like this? Who cares about an old death certificate! Richard, I want you to call the sheriff's office tomorrow and tell them to leave her alone. Mrs. Tuggle has suffered enough over the years without having to be reminded of her brother's death all over again."

Lynn stared at her mother and then at her father. Mother talked as though she were making a speech—as though she had been coached on what to say. Her eyes still held that faraway look and her lips moved mechanically. Mrs. Tuggle had done it already. Obviously she had made a new potion stronger than anything she had given Mother before.

"Go to the sheriff's office tomorrow," she said, "and tell them that there is no point whatsoever in demanding that death certificate. Tell them to just forget about it. And tell them that the old cemetery should stay right where it is. I want you to tell them that too. They'll listen to you. You're on the zoning commission. You have influence."

"Sylvia!" Father said. "What's happened to you? You know I can't interfere like that."

"Just leave that poor woman alone," Mrs. Morley went on, and seemed not even to have heard what Father said. "Just leave her alone. And the grave too."

Lynn got up from the table and looked at the clock in the kitchen. Ten to seven. She got her jacket from the hall closet and a flashlight from the shelf.

"Where are you going, Lynn?" Father called.

"I have to go somewhere with Mouse," Lynn answered. She went outside and shut the door.

Things were moving rapidly now. Mrs. Tuggle was using Mrs. Morley in her own defense, putting words in Mother's mouth.

Mouse was coming up the street, wearing her dark blue coat with the hood. Lynn ran down to meet her.

"How are we going to do it, Lynn? How on earth are we going to do it?"

"I've got it all figured out. Tell Mrs. Tuggle that your father got her note and wants her to come down to the store right now to look over Bertha Voight's old books. As soon as she leaves, we'll crawl in a window or something."

"Lynn, how can I do that? Dad's not even there. He's at home!"

"So much the better. She'll probably stay there awhile waiting for him to come and open up, and by the time she gets back here, we'll have found the box that Judith was telling us about."

"By the time she gets back she'll be ready to kill us, Lynn."

"We'll be gone, Mouse! There won't be a thing she can do."

"Oh, lordie," said Mouse, and her voice quavered again.

When they reached the clump of spruce trees on the corner of Mrs. Tuggle's lot, however, they saw the front door of the old house open, and Mrs. Tuggle came out with a basket over her arm.

"She's going shopping!" Lynn whispered. "Mouse, we're in luck! Hurry! Get in here."

They moved back in the pine trees and crouched down, waiting till the old woman passed. Mrs. Tuggle walked rapidly, as though helped along by the wind— quick and strong and determined. As soon as she was a block away, the girls crept out of the trees and up the brick path to the house.

Lynn felt sure she would be able to open one of the upstairs windows by taking the side steps up to the narrow balcony. It was unnecessary, however, for they discovered that the back door had been left unlocked, not uncommon in this small Indiana town, and the girls walked straight into the dark kitchen without difficulty.

Lynn flicked on the flashlight.

"Don't touch the light switches, Mouse," she cautioned. "If Mrs. Tuggle looks back and sees a light, she'll be right on our necks. Let's go up to the sewing room and look for the box before we do anything else."

They crept through the dark hallway, following the round circle of light—past the grandfather clock that no longer ticked, past the cracked vase, past the coat stand with claws for hooks, till they reached the foot

of the stairway, and began the long climb to the second floor.

The sewing room was at the front of the house, next to the guest bedroom. It was a narrow room with a large closet on one side and a long table in the middle beside Mrs. Tuggle's old treadle sewing machine. There were shelves at one end, over the window, and Lynn's flashlight revealed mending baskets and boxes of ribbon, trays of colored thread and shoe boxes filled with old patterns. On the other side of the room was a rocking chair and a high, dark bureau, just as Judith had said.

It was the tallest bureau the girls had ever seen—mahogany in color, and every drawer had small brass knobs.

"That's it," said Mouse. "That must be the bureau that Judith was talking about." She eased open one of the drawers and Lynn shone the light inside. It was filled with candles, and all of them were black. Mouse shrank back.

"Oh, Lynn, don't!" she cautioned.

"We'll search the bureau later," Lynn agreed. "Let's go for the box."

The problem was that the top of the bureau was far too high to reach. It came within a foot of the ceiling, and there was nothing at all visible from below.

"Help me move the sewing table over, Mouse," Lynn said. "Maybe I can stand on that and reach it from there."

The table was unusually heavy. The girls tugged and

pushed till they got it next to the bureau.

"Gosh, Lynn, I wish we were out of here," Mouse said, going over to the window to watch the street below. "Do people ever die of fright? If Mrs. Tuggle walked in here right now my heart would just give out. I swear it."

"I'll be through in a minute," Lynn promised, standing up on the table. She reached as far as she could, but her hands only came up to the edge of the top of the bureau.

She got back down, put the sewing chair on the table, and climbed on top of that. This time she had to duck her head to keep from hitting the ceiling.

"Hand me the flashlight now, Mouse," she said, and she turned it on the dusty top of the old bureau.

There was the box. It was low and gray, and it had been shoved near the back by the wall, so that it would have been impossible for anyone to see from below, no matter how tall.

"It's here," Lynn whispered, and carefully grasped it in one hand, hugging it to her.

"Oh, Lynn, I don't think I can look!" Mouse bleated as Lynn climbed back down. "What if it's got somebody's fingers in it or something?"

Lynn wasn't sure just what she had expected to see. A sorcerer's ring, perhaps. Or an ancient medal. A book of spells, maybe, or a witch's charm. Gingerly her fingers lifted the hinged lid and she shone the flashlight inside. There lay a piece of white chalk.

"Chalk!" Lynn cried in dismay. "Good grief, all this

work for a piece of chalk!"

Granted, it was an unusually thick piece, not the sort that was used on blackboards in school. But chalk nonetheless. Lynn turned it over and over in her hand, scarcely able to contain her disappointment.

But Mouse stared at it thoughtfully. "Wait, Lynn. I remember something. Something from the book of spells and potions about a consecrated piece of chalk that was able to keep demons away . . . yes, I remember! If you have this chalk—or even a consecrated stick or a sword or something—and you're in the presence of evil, you can draw a circle around yourself and the evil can't get to you. Because if the evilness breaks through the circle, it loses its power."

"Are you *sure*, Mouse?"

"I'm not sure of anything. I just read about it in that old book."

"What's consecrated mean?"

"Blessed or something. A priest says some words over it, maybe."

"How do we know if this is consecrated?"

"We don't. But there must be something special about it or Mrs. Tuggle wouldn't keep it hidden way up there. You know, I'll bet it belonged to Bertha Voight! Maybe this is what she kept in her apron pocket! I'll bet Bertha got it to break Mrs. Tuggle's power in the village. Remember that her brother said she used to go to an old priest? He must have given it to her. Somehow Mrs. Tuggle got the chalk away from her. Old Bertie knew a lot more about Mrs. Tuggle than we do, Lynn. That's why Mrs. Tuggle is so anxious now to go through Bertha's things, now that they've been auctioned off, especially her books and diaries, to see how much she knew, to make sure nobody else finds out."

There was a sound outside. Lynn froze to the floor, her fingers gripping the chalk. Mouse wheeled around and rushed to the window.

"It's Mrs. Tuggle!" she cried. "She's back already! She just closed the front gate!"

chapter eight

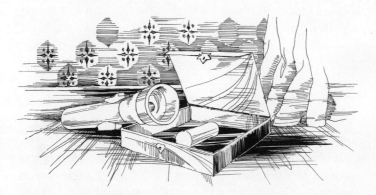

"Go out the back door! Hurry!" Lynn said, hugging the gray box with the chalk tightly against her. They raced down the stairs and started toward the kitchen just as Mrs. Tuggle's head passed by a side window in the moonlight.

"She's coming in the back door!" Mouse bleated, and they tumbled toward the front door. It was bolted, however, and they could not work the lock.

Mouse slumped against the wall. "Lynn, we're trapped!"

In answer, however, Lynn grabbed Marjorie's arm and dragged her toward the cellar door which led off the kitchen. She closed it gently behind them just as Mrs. Tuggle's footsteps sounded on the back steps, and the kitchen door opened.

For a brief moment there was silence, as though the old woman were looking around her, sniffing the air, sounding things out. Then the kitchen light came on, the shopping basket plunked down on the table, and Mrs. Tuggle's footsteps moved into the hallway where she hung up her coat in the closet.

Lynn and Mouse tiptoed on down the basement stairs in the beam of the flashlight and hid behind the great furnace.

"Don't worry," Lynn whispered. "She doesn't know we're here. We'll wait till she goes upstairs to take a bath or something, and as soon as she does, we'll leave."

Then they remembered the table in the sewing room and the chair on top of that. Mrs. Tuggle would know that someone had been in her house. But perhaps she wouldn't discover it right away. Maybe she wouldn't even go into the sewing room till morning. In any case, as soon as they heard her footsteps going upstairs, they would make a run for it.

The cellar was pitch black. Lynn was afraid to keep the flashlight on very long for fear the batteries would wear out. She shone it around just long enough to make out the old trunks and boxes along one wall, the washing machine along another, the shelves of preserves in an adjoining room, and the large open space in front of the furnace.

"This would be great for skateboarding," Lynn quipped, trying to kid Mouse out of her terror. But somehow the very mention of anything happy and normal made their present situation seem all the worse. She wondered if they would ever get out alive, ever have the chance even, to skateboard again.

"Lynn!" Mouse whispered after a moment, panic-stricken. "What if she locks the basement door before she goes to bed?"

Lynn gulped. She hadn't considered that. Many people did lock their basements, in case a burglar came through a cellar window during the night.

"Maybe we'd better make a run for it now, Mouse," she said, moving out from behind the furnace into the open space. "As soon as she puts her groceries away and we hear her go into the living room, let's tiptoe upstairs and go out the back door."

"She'll hear us. . . ."

"We can make it outside, though. Better than being trapped in here all night."

The problem was that there was no sound at all of groceries being put away, and the light went off in the kitchen. If Mrs. Tuggle had gone to market, she hadn't purchased very much. In fact, as Lynn thought about it, Mrs. Tuggle had had barely enough time to go there at all. Perhaps she had just run an errand—taken something to a neighbor.

The girls stood absolutely still in the blackness, straining to hear every sound, desperately trying to sort out the small noises from above. Now there was a creaking in the hallway, the kitchen, then the living room, then the kitchen again. . . . Once they thought they heard footsteps going upstairs, but then there was a noise in the kitchen again. The old woman must be prowling like a cat, everywhere at once. Or perhaps she wasn't moving at all. Perhaps she was sitting in the kitchen in the darkness, waiting for them to come up. And perhaps the creaking was merely the settling of old wood in an old house.

Then, from somewhere above them, came the soft quavery croon of an old woman's voice, singing a tune. But it wasn't a song, really—it was more of a chant, and Lynn remembered that a year ago, when her sister had been under Mrs. Tuggle's spell, Judith used to recite it to herself:

> *"From the shadows of the pool,*
> *Black as midnight, thick as gruel,*
> *Come, my nymphs, and you shall be,*
> *Silent images of me."*

The words were as clear as if they had been uttered in the same room where the girls were standing, as though the voice came drifting in through the large round pipes that fed into the furnace:

> *"Suck the honey from my lips,*
> *Dance upon my fingertips,*
> *When the darkness tolls the hour,*
> *I shall have you in my power."*

"Lynn!" Mouse cried, clutching her friend's arm. Her entire body was shaking. "She means us! Oh, lordie, we'll never get out of here . . ."

The voice went on, rising and falling:

> *"Fast upon us, spirits all,–*
> *Listen for our whispered call,*
> *Whistling kettle, tinkling bell,*
> *Weave your web and spin your spell."*

And then, there was the sound of slow, soft footsteps on the floor above them, but the girls could not make out exactly where they were or where they were going. At the same time, Mrs. Tuggle began talking out loud, every syllable carrying to the basement as though the old woman were floating right through the walls:

"Ah, my pretties, so you've come to see Mrs. Tuggle, eh? 'Tis a fine thing, then, to hide your faces! Maybe my visitors are shy—shy they are to show their faces. Well, old Mrs. Tuggle doesn't mind. Games, eh? That's what they like. Hide and seek. Where are my pretties? In the closet, maybe? No . . . not here. . . ."

"She'll go through every room, Lynn, till she's found us!" Mouse wept. "This is it! Nobody knows we're here, Lynn. No one will ever find us!"

"Shhhhh. She'll hear. If only she'd go upstairs. . . ."

It was plain, however, that the old woman was moving about in the hallway, so that she could keep an eye on both the front and back doors at once.

"Maybe we can fight her off," Lynn said. "Make a run for it and just plow right over her if we have to. There are two of us and only one of her."

137

"Lynn, she's strong! She's strong as an ox! Her arms are like steel."

And then the footsteps seemed to be in the kitchen overhead, coming closer and closer to the basement door.

"Now where could my pretties be hiding?" Mrs. Tuggle crooned from above. "In the cupboards, perhaps? No. . . . In the hall closet? . . . Not here either. . . ."

"Lynn," Mouse said suddenly. "Take the chalk and draw a wide circle around us on the floor, about nine feet in diameter. . . ."

"What?"

"Hurry! It's the only thing left to do. If I'm right about the chalk, she won't be able to step into the circle without losing her power."

"But we won't dare to get out!"

"At least we'll be safe for a while."

"Mouse, are you sure it will work?"

"No, but we've got to try. Oh, Lynn, hurry!"

Lynn took the chalk from the box and, while Marjorie held the flashlight, began drawing a big white line, just as the basement door opened above.

"I wonder if they could be in my cellar," Mrs. Tuggle said, her voice cracking with pleasure and expectation. "I wonder if my pretty little girls could be waiting for me down there?"

One bony hand reached in and felt for the light switch at the top of the stairs. The light came on and Mrs. Tuggle came down a few steps.

Suddenly a terrible shriek filled the basement. Mrs. Tuggle stopped there on the steps, staring at the white line, her eyes huge, her face contorted with fury. Then swiftly she rushed down the steps toward them, arms outstretched, just as Lynn brought the two ends of the circle together. Mrs. Tuggle reeled backwards and shrieked again.

Lynn and Mouse clutched each other in the center of the circle, both of them shaking uncontrollably as Mrs. Tuggle struggled to speak. Her lips moved but no words came out, and her eyes, like fiery coals beneath her heavy brows, glowered with such anger and frustration that Lynn felt surely the old woman would kill them if she could.

"Robbers!" she screamed finally. "You terrible, thieving children! So you have found the chalk, eh, and have protected yourselves, you think. Well, my dears, I am much older and wiser than you believe. Perhaps I cannot get in, but I have ways of drawing you out."

That had not occurred to either of them. She could throw things at them. Hammers, perhaps, or scalding water. She could turn on the faucets till water flooded the basement and forced them up the stairs. But Mrs. Tuggle had something else in mind. She crouched down on her heels like an old beggar woman at a street corner and, putting a finger of each hand on her forehead, began reciting something in another language— a language that sounded far stranger than any Lynn had ever heard in her life. For several minutes the strange recitation went on, till finally Mrs. Tuggle stood up again and, in a loud voice, pointed one finger at Lynn and called:

"Dorolla, I command you to come forward."

At the mention of the name Dorolla, Lynn felt a strange pull, as though her feet were attached to invisible string, and she were being drawn slowly to the edge of the circle. Her eyes, riveted to the eyes of the old woman, saw the ancient face wrinkle into a hideous smile. In horror, Lynn felt the helplessness of her body as it moved without any effort at all on her part.

"Mouse!" Lynn gasped. "Help me!"

"Lynn!" Mouse grabbed Lynn in her arms, but Lynn's other foot lifted and took a step forward, closer to the edge of the chalk circle.

"Come, Dorolla," Mrs. Tuggle said. "I have been waiting for you for a long time. You have resisted me long enough. I have always known you. I know that spirit, which is inside of you and inside of Judith and inside your mother too, for I am their demon superior and it is I who counsels them."

"M . . . Mouse!" Lynn gulped again, as she found herself taking still a third step in spite of herself.

Mouse threw herself on Lynn, knocking her to the floor in order to save her.

"Ah, let her come, my funny little mouse," Mrs. Tuggle said, and laughed like an old hen. " 'Tis your spirit's name I shall call next, and you shall follow after your friend. Quite a chase you have given me, all these months, but now I have you fast. You shall come to Mrs. Tuggle and give me the chalk, for your evilness answers to me."

"Lynn," Mouse wept. "Don't go. Together we can be

stronger than Dorolla could ever be."

"Try what you did last summer in your house, Mouse, when Mrs. Tuggle and all her demons were trying to get in. Sing, Mouse! Sing her song back to her! Throw the evilness back in her face." And shakily, Lynn began to sing the song as even then she was struggling once more to her feet:

> *"From the shadows of the pool,*
> *Black as midnight, thick as gruel . . ."*

Marjorie's voice joined in:

> *"Come my nymphs, and you shall be*
> *Silent images of me . . ."*

It was working. Lynn felt the pull on her lessen, and her feet stopped moving forward. Mrs. Tuggle was scowling, her mouth half open in rage:

"Sevena!" she thundered, pointing her finger at Mouse. "I command you to come forward."

At the mention of the second name, Marjorie, too, struggled to stand up, crawling slowly toward the edge of the circle on her hands and knees.

"Sing, Mouse!" Lynn screamed. "Sing as loud as you can. . . ."

> *"Suck the honey from my lips,*
> *Dance upon my fingertips,*
> *When the darkness tolls the hour,*
> *I shall have you in my power!"*

The last words were interrupted by repeated banging on the big front door upstairs. Mrs. Tuggle whirled around and stared in the direction of the noise. Then she turned and ran up the steps two at a time like a strong animal in its prime.

Soaked in perspiration, trembling with terror, Marjorie and Lynn sank down in the center of the circle, limp. They heard the sound of the front door opening, and then a deep voice saying,

"I've come for my daughter, Mrs. Tuggle."

"Your daughter, Mr. Morley?"

"Yes. I could hear her voice just now. . . ."

"Daddy!" Lynn cried, and ran up the stairs, Mouse at her heels.

Mrs. Tuggle stood rigidly by the big front door, her eyes small with hatred, her bony shoulders jutting up through the cloth of her brown dress.

"Aye, and it's time someone came for the girl and took her in hand!" she declared angrily. "Robbery! That's what she's been up to, Mr. Morley. I found her just now with the Beasley girl in my basement."

Lynn threw her arms around her father, beginning to cry, as Mouse clung to one of Mr. Morley's coat sleeves. Father stared at them in astonishment and confusion.

"Robbery, Mrs. Tuggle?"

"Aye. Never do I want to set eyes on this girl again, Mr. Morley. A disgrace to her dear mother, that's what she is. Take her home and teach her to behave," the old woman snapped.

Father, however, seemed more concerned with the girls.

"Are you all right?" he asked, still staring.

"Now I am," Lynn wept. "Let's go home, Daddy."

"My box!" Mrs. Tuggle demanded.

"We have nothing of yours, Mrs. Tuggle," Lynn said, which was true, for they had left everything behind in the basement.

They started home, one girl on each side of Father, and Mr. Morley had an arm around them both. Would he listen to her now, Lynn wondered. Was this the time to tell him everything?

"Tell me what happened," Mr. Morley said. "What were you doing in her house, Lynn? When you didn't come home, I was afraid that's where you'd gone."

"We were . . . looking for something that would protect Mother," Lynn began.

"Something to protect Mother? What do you mean? You had no right to enter her house like that."

"I know, but I've been so worried."

"Your mother doesn't need any protection now," Father said. "We had a long talk this evening, Lynn. She's promised not to work at Mrs. Tuggle's any more. That woman has a strange influence on our family. I don't understand it, but whatever it is, it hasn't been good. Let's all just stay away from up there and let the sheriff's office finish its investigation."

They walked on a little way in silence.

"But something must have happened back there to

frighten you like this," Father said finally. "When I walked up on the porch, I thought I heard you singing —or screaming—I couldn't tell which."

"She . . . she had us cornered in the basement!"

Mr. Morley looked at Lynn. "Cornered? Was she trying to attack you or something? I need to know honestly, Lynn. Don't go making up stories."

Lynn thought about it. What could she say? "I don't really know what she would have done if you hadn't come to the door just then, Dad. She said she'd been after us a long time, and she was calling us by different names. She said there were spirits inside of us."

"She was obviously upset to find you in her house, and I can't blame her," Father said. "But it does sound to me as though she's becoming mentally unbalanced."

They had reached the steps of the Morley house. "You go on up to bed now, Lynn," Father said. "I'll see that Marjorie gets home. It's a good thing tomorrow's Saturday. I think we all need to sleep late and get some rest. It's been a pretty tense week. You and I are going to sit down and have a long talk about this tomorrow, Lynn."

chapter nine

Lynn slept very little that night. She wished, for one
thing, that she had kept the chalk and brought it home
with her. She would draw a circle around Judith's bed
and Stevie's bed, and around the bed in her parents'
room. She would draw a circle around the whole house,
in fact, and Marjorie's as well. She wished she could
protect them all forever against the evil powers of the
old woman, but she knew that even this would not save
them from the evils in themselves. She was, in part,
Dorolla, a demon, and Mouse was Sevena, and who
knows what names Mrs. Tuggle had given the spirits that
resided in Judith and her mother and the Beasleys and
even little Stevie? Everyone had a second side to his na-
ture, and it was these second selves that Mrs. Tuggle

made it a point to get to know. Even if the trip to the old house hadn't produced anything really useful, it did help some to know just how Mrs. Tuggle operated.

About two o'clock in the morning, it began to rain, hard. Lynn lay between sleep and wakefulness. She remembered thinking once that even if she had drawn a circle around the house, a rain like this one would wash it away. It was the kind of rain one expects in the spring—a heavy rain for fifteen or twenty minutes, gradually tapering off into mist. But this rain did not taper, and by three o'clock, it seemed heavier still, accompanied by fierce winds that shook the third floor bedroom where she and Judith were sleeping.

"Lynn," came Judith's sleepy voice from behind the curtain that separated their spaces, "it sounds as though the house is coming apart! Listen to those shutters banging."

"Mommy!" came Stevie's voice, and then there were footsteps downstairs that told Lynn the whole family was awake. So she put on her angora slippers and her terry cloth robe and went downstairs with Judith.

Mother had Stevie in her arms and was taking him into the kitchen for some hot chocolate, and when they were all seated around the table, Father too came down in his floppy leather sandals.

"Listen to that hail!" he said, as the storm pelted the roof of the back porch. He opened the door and peered out into the night. Every now and then there was a ripping and splitting of tree limbs. "The yard is going to be a sight tomorrow," he said, closing the door again. "This is about the worst thunderstorm I can remember."

"There was one last fall," Mother reminded him. "Remember when part of Mrs. Tuggle's roof came off?"

Lynn remembered. It was the night she and Marjorie had been alone at the Beasleys.

"The weather seems to be changing," Mother went on. "We didn't used to get storms like this in Indiana."

"It sounds like some old wolf is out there huffing and puffing and trying to blow the house down," Stevie said, blowing the marshmallow back and forth over the surface of his cocoa. "Can I sleep in your bed, Daddy?"

"No." Father smiled. "But you may keep your door open, and we'll hear you if you need anything."

The wind died down around four, but the rain continued, dull and steady, with occasional rumbles of thunder in the distance. The family returned to bed.

Maybe the worst is over, Lynn thought, not really thinking of the storm. Everything had seemed so normal back downstairs. Mother had been more like herself, the warm smell of cocoa had been soothing. Maybe now that Mother would be writing at home, Mrs. Tuggle would realize she'd better leave the Morleys alone. Maybe she'd move away, even. That would be better yet.

Lynn dropped off to sleep, but about seven o'clock she was awakened again by someone knocking on the back door. She could hear her father moving about in his room below. She sat up, listened to the footsteps on the stairs, then got up and crept downstairs herself.

Father had opened the back door to Mr. Beasley, who was standing there in an old plaid jacket.

"Sorry to get you up so early on Saturday morning, Dick, but I found something you'd be interested in," he said, stepping into the kitchen. "Went out in my back yard this morning to see what damage the storm had done, and looking out across the field, I could see where that big oak tree on the hill in the old cemetery had been uprooted and fallen down. I went over to take a look and found a skeleton half out of the ground. When the tree was uprooted, it made a deep hole in the earth and brought the Pritchard boy's grave up with it. With all this talk going on about that missing death certificate, I think we ought to call the sheriff. Maybe he'll want to have the skeleton examined."

"I'm glad you came by," Father told him. "I'll get dressed and be out in a few minutes."

Lynn sat around the corner on the bottom step, listening. So there really had been a body. There went her theory about Mrs. Tuggle's turning her brother into a demon cat. Now she didn't know what to think.

Mr. Morley came around the corner and almost stepped on her.

"Good grief, Lynn, what are you doing up so early? I'll bet you heard everything Mr. Beasley said."

Lynn nodded.

"I'm going with him to get the sheriff," he told her. "When Mother wakes up, tell her where I've gone. I've a notion the sheriff will take the skeleton over to the state pathologist in Westburg."

Lynn slowly dressed and went back downstairs to eat a bowl of cornflakes and a doughnut. If there was only a skeleton left, what could a pathologist find out? If there were no broken bones, no gashes on the skull, could a pathologist say that a person had *not* been murdered? It wouldn't really prove a thing. She felt depressed. The pathologist would say he found no evidence of violence; people would stop gossiping about Mrs. Tuggle, and she would be free to go right on working her witchcraft.

Mouse came over before Mrs. Morley was awake, and the two girls sat on the glider out on the back porch, watching the swirling dark clouds out over Cowden's Creek, listening to the steady peal of thunder, like the roll of a drum, and talking about the skeleton of C. L. Pritchard and what would happen next.

About nine o'clock, Mother came downstairs and made some coffee for herself. Lynn told her where Father had gone. Judith awoke too and took Stevie to the library for story hour and a puppet show. Mouse and Lynn waited on the back porch for Father to come back. They were so intent on their talk and speculation that Lynn didn't even notice that Mother herself was getting ready to go outside till she came out on the back porch in her raincoat.

It was not just the fact that Mother was going out that bothered Lynn. It was the agitated way she moved, from one side of the porch to the other, looking out over the fields, then going back in the kitchen to continue her restless pacing.

"I'm worried about her, Mouse," Lynn said finally. "It's as though Mrs. Tuggle is calling her. Do you think she can do that—send out vibrations or something from up there on the hill?"

As if in answer to the question, Mrs. Morley came out on the porch once more.

"Lynn, I simply must have the manuscript here if I'm to finish the book," she said. "I've only one more paragraph to go, and I could finish it this weekend. I promised your father I'd write here at home, so I'm going up to Mrs. Tuggle's to get it. I'll be back shortly."

Lynn sat frozen beside Mouse. The glider stopped rocking. "I . . . I thought you told Dad you wouldn't go up there any more," she said numbly.

"I said I wouldn't *write* there, and I'd like to know how I'm supposed to write here at home without my manuscript!" Mother snapped. "Besides, I need the exercise."

"We'll walk up there with you, then," Lynn offered.

"No, we won't!" breathed Mouse, nudging her in the ribs. "Lynn, we don't dare."

"Not after the trouble you girls got into last night," said Mother. "I am perfectly capable of taking care of myself."

"Promise you'll be right back, then?" Lynn asked.

"In time for lunch. Judith and Stevie should be back by one, and I told them I'd make a pizza. You'll stay and have some with us, won't you, Marjorie?"

"Sure," said Mouse, who never passed up an offer for food.

Mother left, walking briskly up the hill toward the

house at the top. The thunder continued. Now and then a flash of lightning streaked across the sky. Lynn watched her go with foreboding.

"Let's play duets," Mouse said, as if to take Lynn's mind off her fears.

Mouse was behaving more and more like a capable adult herself, Lynn decided as she followed her into the music room. Marjorie seemed to be adjusting much better to the fact that she and her father made up their family now, and that her mother, however much Mouse loved her, would not be as big a part of her life as she had hoped. She made plans for meals, and organized the housework and sometimes helped her father out in his bookstore. She seemed proud, now that she could recover from the shock of the divorce and go on to live a full and happy life, as full and happy, that is, as a life can be in the shadow of Elnora Tuggle.

They sat down together on the piano bench. Mouse took the more complicated bass part and Lynn took the treble. They went through "Chopsticks" and all the other songs they knew, then gave up because Lynn's heart simply wasn't in it.

"How long's she been gone, Mouse?" Lynn asked finally. The clock on the bookcase read eleven.

"About forty minutes."

"How long does it take to walk up the hill, pick up a manuscript, and come home again?"

"They're probably talking. She probably feels she at least has to be polite."

152

"Maybe."

They sat together on the window seat and watched the strange zigzags of lightning. If it continued raining, the business district would probably flood again. Maybe it would even flood as badly as it had forty years ago when houses were washed away, when Mrs. Tuggle's brother and Bertha Voight and two other people had disappeared in the flood. Maybe people always disappeared when it rained. Maybe Mrs. Tuggle waited for a good storm to come along and then got rid of anyone who was in her way. Or maybe she took that opportunity to turn them into demon spirits and put the blame on the flood. Her heart thumped with anxiety again, and she looked at the clock. Eleven-fifteen. Mother had been gone an hour.

The phone rang and she jumped.

"Hello?"

"Hi. Lynn? This is Dad. Mother around?"

"No. She should be back any minute."

"Tell her I won't be home for lunch. I decided to go over to Westburg with the sheriff. Something's come up."

"What did they find, Daddy? You might as well tell me, because you know I'll find out anyway."

There was a pause, then a sigh. "You're right about that," Father said. "Anyway, it'll be in tomorrow's paper, so it's no secret. Well, we've had something of a shock. The skeleton in the Pritchard boy's grave is not that of a boy at all but of a young woman. We're checking the teeth and will compare them with old dental records later to see if we can identify her that way."

Lynn gasped. "Bertha Voight!" she said at once.

"Who?"

"Bertha Voight. Have them check *her* dental records, Dad! I'll bet that's who it is."

"Who's she?" Mr. Morley asked. "How do you know this, Lynn?"

"I'm just sure, Daddy! I know! She disappeared at the same time Mrs. Tuggle's brother did, and she and Mrs. Tuggle were sort of enemies. Oh, Dad! I'm sure! Mrs. Tuggle must have killed her and buried her where her brother was supposed to be!"

"Now, listen." Father's voice seemed shaky itself. "We're going to let the sheriff handle this, Lynn. I'll tell him what you've said, but in the meantime, don't any of you go up to Mrs. Tuggle's. Do you hear? I want you all to stay home till I get there."

"Oh, D . . . Dad!" Lynn gasped again. "Mother's there."

"What?"

"She went up to Mrs. Tuggle's an hour ago to get her manuscript and bring it home, and she said she'd be right back and she's not here!"

"I'm coming home!" Father said. "It'll take twenty minutes or so, but I'm on my way."

He hung up. Lynn discovered she was crying.

"M . . . Mouse," she said, and told her the news at once. "We've got to go after Mother. If Mrs. Tuggle knows about the skeleton being found, she'll work all her magic to keep the sheriff away, and she'll need Mother's help. Dad's so worried he's coming right home."

"Then let him take care of it, Lynn," Mouse begged. "He'll know what to do."

"Mouse! Don't you see? It may be too late! Mrs. Tuggle will know that it's the last time she'll have Mother up there alone! Whatever she's going to try, she'll try now! She could hold her as a sort of hostage. She could keep her there, and tell the sheriff that if he sets foot in her yard, something would happen to Mother! I've got to go up there, Mouse, and get her."

"Lynn, she'll kill you."

"Mouse, please come with me. Wait outside behind the trees, and if I'm not out with Mother in five minutes, go get your father or the police or someone."

"I'm frightened!"

"So am I."

They threw on jackets and ran up the hill to the edge of the spruce trees. The sky was black and churning. It was like dusk, yet it was noon. The wind was growing stronger, and the lightning cracked down on them as though it were demanding the very spot on which they stood.

"F . . . five minutes, then," said Mouse, as Lynn got down on her hands and knees and crawled along the fence toward the gate. "I mean it, Lynn. If you're not back out by then, I'll go for the whole U.S. Army."

It was useless, Lynn knew, to try to enter through a door. The doors would be locked now, and Mrs. Tuggle would certainly not let her in if she knocked. Somehow she had to get upstairs without the old woman knowing.

She made her way on her hands and knees from bush to bush, stopping behind the thornapple tree to stand up and rub her knees, then down on all fours again, ignoring the mud. Inch by inch she made her way along until at last she reached the outside steps that led up to the second floor balcony surrounding three sides of the house, and climbed them.

The floor at the top tilted slightly away from the house, like a listing ship. It was easier to get down on her hands and knees again and crawl along it, sticking close to the wall so she would not be seen going past a window should Mrs. Tuggle be upstairs.

The room where Mother worked was around on the other side, away from the steps. It was necessary first to crawl past the guest bedroom, then the sewing room, and finally turn the corner to arrive at the window of Mother's room.

Down below in the clump of spruce trees, Lynn could see Marjorie's anxious face looking up at her, and wished that Mouse would keep out of sight. If Mrs. Tuggle looked out and saw Mouse standing there looking upward, she would know that something was afoot.

At last she reached Mrs. Morley's room, and slowly raised up, peeping in one corner of the window. Mother was sitting tensely in her chair, still wearing her coat, the manuscript in her lap, looking distraught and frightened.

Lynn tapped lightly on the glass and put one finger

to her lips. Then she pushed open the window.

Mrs. Morley started, her lips parting, staring at Lynn as though not quite sure who she was. Lynn crawled in.

"Come on, Mother," she whispered. "Father wants you to come home."

"I . . . I can't, Lynn," Mother said desperately, and her eyes looked half wild. "I don't know w . . . why, but I can't seem to move out of this chair. I'm like the heroine in my story, trapped in the steeple of a crumbling church. I'm so frightened!"

"Mother, you've got to come! Quickly! I'll help you. Crawl out the window with me."

Mrs. Morley leaned forward as if to stand up, but suddenly slumped backwards again. "I can't, Lynn," she said, her voice trembling. "I just can't. I'm trapped by my own words. It's as though the same spell I've been writing about has taken over me."

"Then *write*, Mother!" Lynn pleaded. "Write that she escaped! Just put down those words!"

Mother reached out and shakily picked up her pen. Her hand shook so she could scarcely hold it, but somehow she managed to produce six words:

And . . . so . . . Dorolla . . . let . . . her . . . go.

Lynn gasped. That name! How could Mother know it? Somehow Mrs. Tuggle had controlled them all— even the book that Mother had been writing.

The pen fell out of Mrs. Morley's hand and onto the desk, and Mrs. Morley stood up. Still, however, her other hand gripped the arm of the chair.

"I can't, Lynn!" Mother said again, weeping. "I can't

157

seem to let go! Whatever is the matter with me?"

There was another crack of thunder. This time it was so loud that Lynn felt sure she had been hit. It was like an explosion that rocked the room, yet when it was over, nothing seemed out of place. The room looked as it always had. And then she heard Mouse screaming from outside.

"Fire! Fire!"

At the same moment she smelled smoke and heard a crackling noise on the roof. Lightning had hit the house.

"Mother! The house is on fire!" Lynn said. "Come on!"

"I can't, Lynn! I can't let go! Run, Lynn! Get out while you can! Don't wait for me!"

Lynn knelt down beside her mother to see if she could work her fingers loose from the arm of the chair. As she did so, her knee scraped something sharp. She looked down. The cat's chain, the spider medallion, had been twisted around and around one rung.

Swiftly Lynn unwrapped it and flung it out the open window to the ground below. Instantly her mother's fingers relaxed, and Mrs. Morley was able to move at last. The smoke became more dense, and the noise of the fire above them was becoming a roar.

There were rapid footsteps on the stairs coming up.

Lynn yanked her mother toward the window. Mrs. Morley climbed out, Lynn behind her, just as Mrs. Tuggle burst into the room.

The old woman gave a shriek, and lunged toward them, grasping at Lynn's coat.

But Lynn jerked free and ran with her mother around the balcony and down the side steps just as a car pulled up in front and Father bounded out. No sooner had they reached the bottom than there was a sudden whoosh, like a gust of wind, and the whole upper story of the old house was engulfed in flames.

Mr. Morley was holding Mother in his arms, and Lynn and Mouse crouched together behind them, their faces buried in their hands. They heard the sirens coming up the hill from the village below. They heard the roar of the trucks and the shouts of the firemen, the running of feet and the rushing of water. They heard the horrified voices of neighbors gathering out beyond the gate, and the cracking and falling of timber as bit by bit the old house caved in. When at last they forced themselves, white and shaken, to lift their heads and look, there was nothing left but the big stone fireplace where the parlor had once been, and ashes all around.

The swollen water of Cowden's Creek had receded, leaving only a damp line along the bank. The fallen oak tree in the old cemetery had been hauled away by a maintenance crew, which was transferring all the coffins to their new location on the east side of town. But the other trees would be left standing. Picnic tables would take the place of tombstones when the spot became a wooded park for the whole town to enjoy.

This particular Saturday, unlike the Saturday of the fire, a month earlier, was calm and quiet, with large puffy clouds in a blue sky, daffodils in profusion, and a warmth in the air that meant jackets and coats were not needed. After four weeks of saying that they would go back up there "some day," Lynn and Mouse gathered up the courage and set out for the house on the hill, or the place where the house had once been. Mr. Beasley was working in the bookstore, Judith had gone hiking with a boyfriend, Stevie was at a birthday party, Mr. Morley was washing the car, and Mother was baking bread and going over the details of a new book in her head.

There would be no more books about witches. The manuscript—the one that Mrs. Morley had been working on for a year—had been left behind in Mrs. Tuggle's house and had burned along with the old woman who had inspired it. Lynn had thought that Mother would be devastated at the loss of a year's work, but Mrs. Morley seemed at peace for the first time in many months.

"I feel so different," she had told Father recently. "What a terrible way for it all to end, and yet I am so glad to be rid of that book. I was possessed, Dick. It's as simple as that."

It felt good to be going somewhere with Marjorie without being afraid, Lynn thought—afraid of the demon cat that watched them from the bushes or the crows overhead, or the quick form of Mrs. Tuggle bearing down on them swiftly from out of nowhere. The witchcraft that had affected them all, in one way or another, had been buried along with Mrs. Tuggle's bones three weeks ago.

Mr. and Mrs. Beasley were not getting back together, however. Witchcraft may have been responsible for many things, but the Beasley divorce was not one of them. Life would have been very simple, Lynn decided, if everything that went wrong could be blamed on the witches. But you couldn't do that. There were problems inside people that would always cause trouble whether Mrs. Tuggle was around to draw the evilness out or not. Witchcraft was not responsible for Lynn teasing Stevie or Mouse goofing up a piano lesson. There was still a real world to come back to even after the death of the old woman.

The girls reached the clump of spruce trees in the corner of the now vacant lot, their tips still black and singed from the heat of the fire. The house was gone, of course, and the barn, and half the tractor shed. The henhouse studio, where Mother once wrote, was black on one side, but otherwise all right. No one, however, had come up here since the fire except the inspectors, and once they had searched the grounds and made their reports, they were happy to leave the charred remains to the field mice, which had moved in and claimed the old fireplace as their home.

But Lynn knew she had to come. She had to walk over every inch of the place where the house had once stood. She had to recite the name of her own demon, Dorolla, again and again to familiarize herself with it so that it could never again creep up unexpectedly and take her by surprise. She had to be convinced finally and firmly that she, Lynn Morley, was in control of her life.

"Well, this is it!" Mouse said, as they reached the edge of the charred wood that lay in heaps inside the foundation.

They lowered themselves down into the open cellar where the rubble lay, and stood by the remains of the big furnace, remembering the last time they had stood there. How close they had both come, Dorolla and Sevena, to giving in. . . .

"Maybe if she had lived, she would have given up witchcraft eventually," Lynn said thoughtfully. "People do change, you know. Maybe, if it hadn't been for her fears about what might happen if they discovered the body of Bertha Voight, she wouldn't have tried to start a coven again and build up her cone of power."

"I wouldn't be too sure," said Mouse. "Remember that her brother was still hanging around as the demon cat. Of course, he was only a cat for a while. What do you suppose he was before that? A crow, a rat, an owl, maybe? That's why his body was never found. She was always transforming it."

They continued to walk around, turning over little bits of rubble with their shoes, a piece of a teacup, a curtain rod. . . .

"Does your father believe you now?" Mouse asked finally.

Lynn looked at her. "Does yours?"

They both smiled.

"I guess they never will," said Mouse. "Daddy says that Mrs. Tuggle controlled a lot of people because they *wanted* to be controlled, that in one way or another, they were ripe for it."

"My father doesn't even try to explain it," Lynn said. "He just says he's glad we're all back again. That's what he told Mother last night."

Suddenly Lynn stopped and leaned over to look at something in the ashes.

"Mouse, look here."

It was the cat's chain, with the spider medallion, charred and burned almost beyond recognition. When Lynn picked it up, it fell apart in her hand.

"This place gives me the creeps," Mouse said, shuddering. "Let's go." She turned and started climbing back over the rubble.

Lynn started to follow, then stopped. Something else had caught her attention—something that gleamed at her from under a fallen beam. She knelt down. It was a green glass eye.

She backed away, then returned, drawn to it and repelled both at the same time. She had always wondered why Mrs. Tuggle had one gray eye and one green one. This was all that was left of the old woman now.

As she stared at it, the eye, for just a moment, seemed to wink at her. Lynn stood up and quickly ran after Mouse. When she got to the foundation wall, however, she turned. The eye winked again—one more time— and then went dull. Lynn crawled up the concrete blocks and hurried away. She did not look back at all.

78 81 86
82
84 88 98

DATE DUE

JUN 2 2 1999

Please do not remove this card from pocket

GAYLORD 143